Praise for Sarah Granger's *A Minor Inconvenience*

"...this romance is one of the best period pieces I've ever read. It's obvious that Sarah has done her research. [...] I highly recommend this story to those who enjoy historical romances, handsome, sexy men, suspense, intrigue, and mystery. Thank you, Sarah, for a truly entertaining piece."

~ *Rainbow Book Reviews*

"All in all I loved this book...I think anyone who loves historical romance written in the style of its setting and who likes a plot based story will love it too."

~ *Mrs Condit & Friends Read Books*

"I applaud the author for delivering a fresh, captivating plot and such wonderfully unique characters as Hugh and Theo. If you are fancying a highly entertaining historical story—you can't go wrong here."

~ *Live Your Life, Buy the Book*

"I just loved the way this book read; like reading a gay Jane Austen. The style of writing and setting was perfect for a Regency style MM romance."

~ *Sinfully Sexy Book Reviews*

A Minor Inconvenience

Sarah Granger

Samhain Publishing, Ltd.
11821 Mason Montgomery Road, 4B
Cincinnati, OH 45249
www.samhainpublishing.com

A Minor Inconvenience

Print ISBN: 978-1-61922-308-0
Digital ISBN: 978-1-61921-766-9

Editing by Amy Sherwood
Cover by Kim Killion

First Samhain Publishing, Ltd. electronic publication: January 2014
First Samhain Publishing, Ltd. print publication: January 2015

Dedication

To Leonie,
For your friendship, for the fun and the laughter,
and for the way it always comes back somehow to breeches.

Chapter One

Hugh paused on the landing, allowing himself a moment to regain his breath after mounting the stairs. Matthews, as was his way these days, had found something that required his attention in the hall before following Hugh up the staircase. By the time Matthews opened the door to the drawing room to announce him, Hugh had recovered from the climb.

"A glass of sherry, Captain Fanshawe?" Matthews asked as Hugh entered the room.

"Thank you," Hugh said with feeling. Not only did Matthews know his habits, but he understood the very real needs of a man about to face his mother and younger sister, both of whom would be full of excitement about the evening revelry to come.

The curtains in the spacious room had been closed against the dark March evening, and in the light cast by the many candelabra around the room, the diamonds at his mother's throat glittered. With some bemusement, Hugh observed that Sophia's ivory gown also appeared to sparkle in the candlelight. His dutiful greeting was lost in the excited broadside which she let loose when she saw him.

"Hugh, tell me, what do you think? I believe it is quite the loveliest gown I have ever had!" Sophia spun round, allowing Hugh to admire the gown's full magnificence. "It is spider gauze with silver roses embroidered upon it, and pearls too, and it's so beautiful that I am sure even *George* could not disapprove if he were to see it."

"It's splendid, Sophia," Hugh assured her, all the while hoping that George would not see the gown in question. He did not share Sophia's innocent trust in their brother's reaction. Since becoming Lord Fanshawe and taking his seat in the House of Lords, George had adopted a seriousness of manner which was somewhat at odds with Sophia's joyous approach to purchasing fripperies with no thought for the cost. The handsome estate George had inherited from their father was very well able to bear such outgoings, but he cared not for frivolity.

His mother was surveying Sophia with an indulgent eye as Hugh took his seat upon the sofa. Matthews brought him his sherry, and Hugh noticed the glass was filled more generously than usual. His heart sank. That could not mean anything good lay ahead of him.

"Your sister looks particularly fine tonight, don't you think, Hugh?" His mother was almost as excited as Sophia. "I shouldn't be surprised if the Marquess were to ask her to stand up with him."

Hugh nodded. "You will break many a heart tonight, Sophia—you may depend upon it."

"Oh, Hugh," she said, her face glowing. She came to sit beside him and took his hand into the clasp of her own. "You know I have no interest in breaking hearts, merely in capturing one, but you are the very best of brothers."

Sophia had always had a particular fondness for him. Since his injury at Salamanca, it had found greater and more frequent expression, and he couldn't be quite sure if it made his lot easier or harder to bear. But there was never pity in her eyes, and for that he could weather any number of protestations of love and affection, sincerely meant.

"Oh, *Hugh.*" His mama's voice followed fast upon Sophia's, but her tone was as different from Sophia's as it was possible to be—disappointment and exasperation combined. "Why are you not in your regimentals? You know that the ladies' fondness for them is your only chance now of attracting a wife with anything to recommend her."

"Mama!" Sophia jumped to her feet. "That is quite untrue! And unkind too. Hugh would make the very best of husbands. Any lady would be lucky to have him."

"Of course she would," his mother said swiftly, "but Hugh knows what I mean—the ladies' fondness for a scarlet coat will often carry the day when all else is lost."

Hugh blessed Matthews' prescience as he found refuge in his glass. It was always best with his mother to allow her to run her course—opposing her in any of her beliefs was akin to engaging in a forlorn hope. But no matter the scolding that came his way, he did not regret his decision to dress in a simple waistcoat of watered silk and a black swallow-tailed coat to go with his knee breeches and silk stockings. His choice meant he could fade into the background in a way that the scarlet of his uniform coat would never allow.

Seeking to distract his mother from her focus upon his failings, Hugh asked after the previous evening's entertainment that she had attended and found himself nodding at suitable intervals as he was regaled with a detailed recital of the entire evening. The level in his glass lowered rather swiftly, but the inestimable Matthews rectified that fact with equal swiftness.

Sophia attempted to look interested in the conversation but was all too clearly still taken with her new gown, and she moved to the door with unbecoming haste when his mother finally indicated that it was time to remove to the Fitzroys, who were hosting a ball that night. A ball at which, apparently, the Marquess of Esdale was due, hence the excitement displayed by Hugh's mother. While Sophia was beautiful, she had neither rank nor fortune enough to tempt the Marquess into matrimony, but there was no gainsaying his mama when she had her heart set upon something.

Not for the first time, Hugh thanked the Almighty that, of all the things that had resulted from his injury, one was an almost complete cessation of his mother's attempts to marry him to a suitable heiress. "Had you been either of your brothers," she had confided to him when he had recovered from the arduous journey from Spain to London and had been once more in full possession of his senses, "then your unsoundness would not matter so much, but with only a competence to call your own, and having inherited your dear father's looks, you will be quite unable to attract any young lady of means."

George had inherited the title and the estate, and Hugh's second brother, James, had his mother's vivacious manner and good looks to recommend him to the ladies of the *ton*. Sophia too had taken after their mother; she was the absolute image, apparently, of Lady Fanshawe as she had been at that age. Hugh, on the other hand, had his father's ungraceful solidity as well as his firm jaw—obstinate, his mother had called it when she was adjuring Hugh to go into the church rather than the army. His green eyes and straight fair hair did not please her either, for they contrasted too sharply with the blue eyes and chestnut curls that George, James and Sophia sported.

As if those disadvantages were not enough, he had returned from the war with a leg that would no longer work satisfactorily, resulting in his steps being lame and sometimes, when the pain was very bad, halting. In short, he was now unlikely to attract any of the ladies of even modest fortune that his mama had decided upon for him. Unlike James, of course, who had swept off her feet an accredited beauty with a significant fortune who had, contrary to all Hugh's expectations, turned out to be an intelligent lady who appeared to be very fond of James. They were to be married when he was next on leave.

Regardless of his inability to secure a wife with anything to recommend her, his mother was still keen for Hugh's escort.

George was far too serious and important a man these days to give in to her importuning and allow himself to be dragged through the dreary round of pleasure that was the London Season, and James was still campaigning with Wellington overseas—and for an instant, Hugh allowed himself a moment of envy at that thought. That left Hugh. He had disappointed and distressed his mother by returning home from the Peninsula with such an injury, and he found himself unable to sadden her further her by declining every one of the multitude of invitations she showered upon him. So it was that he was set for an evening which would be composed of almost everything he hated and would rather avoid.

Upon arrival at the Fitzroys' townhouse, he steeled himself for the ascent of the long, curving staircase. Sophia fussed with her reticule in the hall for a time, allowing another group of guests to sweep past them and up the staircase before she pronounced herself ready. Hugh took hold of the banister and began to mount the stairs, secure in the knowledge that for now, he would be delaying no other guests, nor would he suffer the indignity of being passed on the stairs, his halting progress noted with pity or derision.

He was, however, keenly aware of his mother hot upon his heels and an exasperated sigh that she could not quite keep to herself when his progress slowed further as he neared the top of the long flight. Colour flared high in his cheeks as he heard Sophia hiss, "*Mama.*" But then cool, low tones graced his ear, and he knew he was saved.

"Lady Fanshawe, what a delightful surprise it is to see you."

"Lady Emily, I did not know you were coming tonight. Have you seen Sophia's new gown? It is by Madame Lucille, you know—she is the most discerning mantua-maker, and the instant she saw Sophia, she all but begged to be allowed to dress her, for she could see how Sophia takes after me."

Distracted by talk of feminine frills and fashions, his mother ceased to notice the time it took them to ascend to the delights of the ballroom.

Having safely gained the flat terrain of the landing, he turned and greeted Lady Emily d'Arcourt. She was looking ravishing as ever in a crimson velvet gown trimmed with lace that had Sophia staring in open yearning, but it was the warm friendship in her hazel eyes that Hugh most appreciated. She was sister to his best friend at Eton, Lord Robert Trevelyan, and she had been a hoydenish miss who had trailed after the boys wherever they went when Hugh had stayed at Marcham during school holidays. Robert's death at Talavera nearly four years ago had, if anything, brought them closer together, following swiftly as it had upon the heels of her loss of her husband, Chevalier d'Arcourt. Julien d'Arcourt had been many years Lady Emily's senior, but theirs had been a love match, surprisingly unopposed by her parents who might have been expected to object to having an émigré of minor consequence allied with their daughter. Or perhaps, knowing Lady Emily's strong will, she had managed to persuade them into agreement. Whichever the case, he knew that she had truly mourned her husband and had no interest in marrying again. It did not prevent her from attending a goodly number of balls and other revelries for the sake of amusement.

"I'm surprised to see you at yet another ball, Hugh," she confided to him as he joined her later. She was fanning herself lightly to recover from the many dances in which she had engaged. "I hadn't thought they were to your liking."

"It's due to Lady Fanshawe," he confessed as he handed her a glass of iced punch. "She is always so eager for my company upon her excursions and I haven't the heart to refuse her every time."

She took a sip of her punch and looked round the room, apparently casual but in reality, as Hugh knew well, taking in everything with one swift glance. "And it has nothing to do with Sophia's infatuation?"

He stiffened slightly. He had not known Sophia had been so unbecoming as to allow anyone outside the family to know of her feelings for Sir Ralph Stanton. Despite possessing a long line of respectable forbears, he had turned out to be a rackety sort of a fellow, and in Hugh's opinion wholly untrustworthy with young ladies.

"Don't worry," Emily said quietly. "She looks upon me as an aunt, I believe, and confessed all to me when I took her up in my barouche in Hyde Park and we espied him there."

"I know she is perfectly sensible in all other ways," he said, "yet he is entirely unsuitable. It worries me."

"It is scarcely unusual for young girls to form a violent attachment, but do not concern yourself overmuch, Hugh—it seldom lasts."

An unimaginable thought crossed his mind. "Don't tell me you too succumbed at her age," he said, a laugh in his voice. "I will not believe it."

Delicate pink touched her cheeks as she sipped her drink. "Even I, paragon of all things sensible, was not entirely immune," she admitted. "But I soon realised that my feelings were not, and never would be, returned."

"He must have been touched in the head," Hugh declared.

"I think rather that his interest lay elsewhere," she said, surveying the crowded room. "And perhaps Sophia's trouble will dissipate even sooner than you think, because Sir Ralph has none of the address of the gentleman who has just been presented to her. That is a Rifles uniform, is it not?"

Hugh was taken by surprise, for he had not noticed anything other than the usual parade of young misses in their best gowns and exquisitely dressed gentlemen attempting to gain their favour. As he followed Emily's gaze, he could see the dark green of a Rifles uniform, although the angle meant he could see little of the face of the dark-haired colonel wearing it, other than the impression of a firm jawline and smooth cheek. Emily was right—the man's air of address and composure was striking, and as the dance began, Hugh saw he moved not only with grace but also the suggestion of leashed power. He turned away, unwilling to watch any longer and torment himself with what he could never have.

"There is a young lady over there who has been very badly treated by our hostess," Emily said. "No gentleman has yet been presented to her, and she looks as if she wishes to fade into the wallpaper in mortification. Will you rescue her, Hugh?"

"You know I can't," he said. Bitterness edged his voice. He did not expect such casual cruelty from Emily.

"I did not mean you to dance with her," she said steadily, "but I'm sure she would like a handsome young gentleman to procure for her a glass of lemonade."

Shame washed over him. He knew Emily better than that, but being in public like this left him overly conscious of his shortcomings. "Of course," he said, giving her a small smile by way of apology. He escorted Emily to her seat, whereupon she gained the attention of their hostess and enjoined her to present Hugh to the young lady who appeared to be shrinking further into her lonely corner by the instant.

Miss Williams blushed bright pink when Hugh was presented to her. It was not a becoming look, because her hair, strewn through with white flowers, was a vivid red. The smile she summoned at his offer of a glass of lemonade looked like the expression a rabbit caught in a trap might turn upon the gamekeeper who turned up to dispatch it. She had stared in unguarded surprise at his limp as he had approached her, and Hugh thought she would rather have been left to the humiliation of being overlooked than be rescued by someone so lacking.

As he escorted Miss Williams around the edge of the ballroom so that they might go to the supper room, Hugh could not help glancing across the room. Sophia's cotillion with the Rifles officer was continuing, and his first impression of the gentleman's grace and strength was reinforced as he watched. Recalling his manners, he began to make laborious conversation with Miss Williams, who seemed almost too overcome to speak to him, except in rushes of self-conscious gabble. From these, he learned she was from Portsmouth and had come to London for her first Season because there were five daughters to marry off, and everything was bigger and more confusing than she could ever have imagined, and how was she to know just which haberdashers to bestow her custom upon when there were so very many, not at all like Portsmouth. At that, inspiration struck Hugh.

"Shall I introduce you to my sister, Miss Williams? I venture she knows everything there is to know about shops, and I am quite sure that nothing would give her greater pleasure than to share her knowledge."

"Oh, that would be—would it not be an imposition, Captain Fanshawe?" she asked, and for the first time, Hugh could see the beginnings of beauty in her, as her blue eyes sparkled with shy excitement.

They returned to the ballroom to find the cotillion over and Sophia seated once more, a glass of ratafia in her hand. Once he had presented Miss Williams to Sophia, he asked about her dance partner.

"That was Colonel Lindsay," she said carelessly. "He is just back from the war and was interested to hear of you and James. I mentioned you were here, so perhaps he might seek you out if he is not too busy dancing. He is a very charming and graceful partner, so I am sure he will be much in demand, even if he is a trifle old."

Hugh had already seen that the man was graceful; the discovery that Colonel Lindsay was charming did not somehow surprise him. He also knew that anyone above the age of twenty-five was considered old by Sophia. The figure he had seen had the appearance of a man of action who was in his early thirties, five years or so older than Hugh himself, who teetered on the edge of what Sophia might consider acceptable rather than a completely ancient decrepit.

Leaving Sophia to talk ribbons and lace with Miss Williams, Hugh did his duty, circling the room to be introduced as necessary, although no one could fail to notice he was scarcely in demand these days. It gave him the opportunity to search for the dark green uniform, but to no avail. Neither was any sign of Colonel Lindsay to be found in the card room nor the supper room. The only comfort to be found was in Stanton's absence, meaning that as the evening wore on, Hugh felt he no longer needed to watch over Sophia but could retreat to the quieter atmosphere of the card room, where he was drawn into a game of whist. Although that passed the time tolerably, he was thankful when his mama and Sophia finally decided they had enjoyed enough merriment for one evening and that it was time to return home.

He was not looking forward to the carriage ride because he knew Sophia would be disappointed by Stanton's failure to appear. As it happened, he was mistaken—Miss Williams had turned out to be a wonderful companion and Sophia was certain they would soon be the best of friends, and her pleasure at that thought seemed to banish all thoughts of Stanton. As Sophia chattered gaily, Hugh tried to drive from his mind the recurring image of a powerful body in a Rifles uniform. He was not entirely successful.

Chapter Two

Hugh came slowly awake, aware of wind-blown rain rattling against the window of his room and a fire burning brightly in the grate. He pulled the bedclothes higher over his shoulders and sighed contentedly. It was impossible not to think of how fortunate he was to be back in England, with all the comforts of home around him. Even the steady ache from his leg wasn't enough to outweigh being warm, dry and clean, in a comfortable bed and not surrounded by hundreds of men, at least half of whom at any one time were struck down with some sort of fever or other illness. Hugh had been fortunate enough to escape the privations of most of those illnesses. The only time a bad fever took him was after he had been injured, one of his lower leg bones smashed into pieces by a musket ball. Had the ball broken both bones, or had it been but inches higher, the surgeon would have taken his leg and with it, in all probability, his life.

He turned over in the bed, and that was when his leg made its unhappiness with the previous evening's events fully known to him. He hissed and froze, willing the pain to die down. It always did eventually. It wasn't this bad all of the time. He could walk some distance without difficulty, but stairs caused him hardship, and standing for most of a very long night had been a further ordeal. He could have seated himself in the ballroom, but a sense of pride had stopped him, for he refused to be watched by gossiping members of the *ton* having to struggle clumsily from his chair. At Horse Guards, where they were used to relics of war, most people seemed not to notice. That was one of the things he liked most about his duties there.

Other aspects, however, were beginning to cause him concern, and he hoped that James would be granted leave soon so that he might discuss those with him.

Hugh was certain that it was due to George's contacts in the War Office that he'd been given the position at Horse Guards when it became clear he could no longer fight. At first he'd been pleased he could continue in the war against Napoleon, but four months after having first reported to Horse Guards, he was no longer sure that what he was set to do was as helpful as he had originally imagined. Headquarters seemed to be waging their own war against Wellington, placing officers according to seniority rather than competence and approving leave requests without any reference to Wellington's requirements. As he rose from his bed to dress before reporting to Horse Guards, he hoped yet again that he was mistaken in thinking that to be the case.

That afternoon, he was alone in the office he shared with a captain in the 52nd Foot, compiling a list of leave requests for Colonel Dalrymple.

A drawling voice interrupted his concentration. "Fanshawe, must you *really* report at such an ungodly hour in the day? It makes the rest of us look such frippery fellows."

He looked up to see Captain Francis Courtenay leaning in the doorway, regarding him plaintively. Courtenay unpeeled himself from the doorframe. "But I should not complain. I expect you have discharged at least half of this office's work already, leaving me at a loose end."

Hugh blinked down at the paperwork on his desk and realised it was true. He'd had a very definite need for distraction today, because whenever he allowed his mind to wander, thoughts of a strong yet graceful figure in a Rifles uniform kept intruding.

He split the paperwork on his desk into two piles and pushed one of them towards Courtenay. "I would not deprive you further for the world."

"Damn it, Fanshawe. There's no need to be quite so literal, you know."

"I know," Hugh said. "But it amuses me."

Courtenay snorted as he picked up the pile of papers and transferred them to his own desk, situated on the other side of their office. "You are too easily amused, it seems to me. You need more excitement in your life."

"I don't know how I could bear any greater excitement than leave requests," Hugh said. "Truly. They render me positively giddy."

"You should come with me one night to Covent Garden. I warrant you would learn there what excitement really means."

Hugh cursed the slight blush that he knew rose to his cheeks, and which caused Courtenay to laugh at him. He was no innocent—he had been to more than one bawdy house in his time, but since Spain, something had changed. He knew precisely what it was. He did not, however, know what to do about it.

Busying himself with the top sheet of the papers that remained in front of him, Hugh found himself staring unseeingly as he attempted to quiet the restlessness that Courtenay's careless words had set loose in him again, mixing thoughts of carnal pleasure with those of the Rifles colonel from last night. It left him unsettled and wanting.

While campaigning, he had stayed clear of the camp followers, knowing the risks of disease and not seeming to possess the same appetite as other men that drove them to frequent indulgence. He never had been that way; sometimes it worried him that he was different, yet being so saved him from spending his pay on whores from whom he might get the pox, so he failed to see it as too grave a disadvantage.

What had happened at Albuera had changed that. It had changed everything. The battle had been the very worst of all the battles he had been in. It still haunted him sometimes, the sight of whole regiments slaughtered, lying dead in their ranks as they had stood, and the horrible, bloody fate of the Light Brigade in a wild hailstorm that had come from the very depths of Hell.

Three days after the battle, three days of bringing in the dead who seemed to outnumber the living, of hearing the screams of men beneath the surgeons' saws, he was half-mad with the need for it to stop, for a distraction, for the comfort of another living person. He had visited one of the ramshackle tents that the camp followers had erected, and had no problem making his wishes known. A dark-haired woman, who told him her name was Maria, had taken him to her own musty-smelling tent, which had water stains around the seams and looked as if it was home to many more than just her. He had held her close to him, feeling the press of her breasts under her chemise against his uniform and the curve of her hips beneath his hands. He had buried his face in her hair and closed his eyes as he breathed deep and slow, willing everything else away.

He'd opened his eyes again in confusion when she pulled back gently. When he would have asked, she placed a finger on his lips and called quietly for someone named Danilo. A young man had come to her call, with curly hair and smiling brown eyes, and to Hugh's consternation he had found himself taken by the wrist by Danilo and led into the woods behind the camp.

He would not normally have acceded so quietly or easily to he knew not what, but his heart was thundering, the blood rushing through his veins so loud he fancied anyone within five miles could hear it. When the young man stopped, he turned to

Hugh and stepped in close, his breath gusting softly against Hugh's neck as he pressed his body close. At the feel of him, Hugh's breath shuddered out of him in something close to a groan.

Danilo had let go of his wrist, placing one hand on Hugh's chest where the pounding of his heart seemed likely to shake him apart, and his other hand glanced over the fall of his breeches. Hugh had been unable to suppress his moan at the light touch where he needed it so badly. Danilo said something in Spanish and unfastened Hugh's breeches before going to his knees.

It had taken no time at all for things to be over, for Hugh to be fastening his breeches again and giving Danilo some coins before staggering dazedly back to his bivouac. Any mouth on him would have been enough with how he had felt that night, but the way his entire body had reacted, the jolt that had gone through him at the feel of Danilo's hard, very male body pressed to his, left him confused and overwhelmed. The world was falling apart around him, wrenched end from end and put back in a way that could never be the same again, because *that* was what he wanted. And he wanted more of it.

After that, he had gone looking for Danilo several times. He began to notice some of his fellow soldiers in that way, though he quickly schooled himself into not doing so. As he watched the world around him with new eyes, he became aware that there were several boys like Danilo among the camp followers, and that trysts between soldiers, if not precisely commonplace, took place often enough for it to be known.

On his return to London, however, everything changed. It was not only that such a thing was not acknowledged anywhere in polite company, but that indulging in the vice carried with it severe risks. He had put from his mind all thought of being with another in that way, for it was not worth what might follow. But then there had been that damned Rifles officer. Strength and beauty had been in every line of his body, leading Hugh to wish for nothing more than to be held down by him and—

Well, he was not entirely sure what else would happen, but he knew that he would enjoy it.

From conversations in which his men had regularly engaged, he was intimately familiar with the areas of London in which whores, both male and female, might be bought either for money or for wine, and he had also heard jokes about the molly houses in the Strand and St George's Fields. He attempted to put those thoughts from his mind, for he knew the potential for disaster should he weaken and yield to those longings.

But as the afternoon wore on, the idea took hold of Hugh. It would not let him go even as he dined alone in his chambers, his usual practice. The need he felt grew increasingly insistent as he dipped rather more deeply than usual into the Tokay he favoured with his dinner now that French wines were no longer allowed. Once he had drained a third glass of port, he found his decision had been made. His only other option was to continue as he had been, with no relief save from his hand and no intimacy, ever. Danilo, and the others who had followed, had scarcely been intimate, but still it had been less lonely, having someone with whom to share the act.

Two hours and several more glasses of port later, Hugh hesitantly pushed open the door to a coffeehouse on the Strand, unsure if he was in the right place. He thought perhaps not, for he entered into a small vestibule in which there were two men who reminded him in stature and manner of prizefighters.

"Forgive my intrusion," Hugh said. "I was not quite sure— I was— That is to say..." As he stammered into nothingness, he wondered what had happened to the captain who was accustomed to commanding an entire company and leading his men confidently into battle.

He found himself the object of close scrutiny before one of the men jerked his head at the door beyond the vestibule. "On you go, then."

Perhaps this was the right place after all. Hugh's heart was thumping as he pushed open the door, and all doubt vanished.

"Step in, boy, and let the door close," he was adjured.

He did so automatically, because his brain was no longer functioning. What seemed at first glance like a usual coffeehouse, the air filled with tobacco smoke and overly loud conversations amid raucous laughter, was the furthest thing from a usual coffeehouse he could possibly imagine. There were men seated close beside one another, closer than he had ever seen before. Some were touching one another, and others... Others were kissing.

He looked away in confusion, only for his eyes to fall on a gentleman dressed in a rose-pink gown, seated upon another man's lap. He was not just allowing the hands that slid beneath the dress, but he was positioning himself to welcome them. Hugh's stomach swooped at the sight, and he looked away, his eyes fastening on the fire which burned so brightly in the fireplace, making the room uncomfortably warm. It was the only safe thing here. He was not able to recover his equilibrium before a fellow with a quizzing glass approached him, impertinently eyeing him up and down and providing his companions with a running commentary on what he found so interesting in the spread of Hugh's coat across his shoulders and the fit of his pantaloons.

Hugh did not know what to do—one instinct told him to retreat, yet he knew this might be his only chance to find what he wanted. He stood frozen, torn between looking at everything, and at nothing, and then something drew his attention to a corner he had not yet dared look towards.

A man was leaning against the wall, his arms folded as he watched Hugh. Not that this was a particular novelty, for many of the occupants of the coffeehouse appeared to be observing him and deriving amusement from watching him flounder, but this man... His grey eyes were steady on Hugh's face, and it was as if he were stripping Hugh of all he was, seeing right inside him. His dark hair was swept back from his face, his lips were slightly parted, and it hit Hugh with the force of a cannonball that he wanted this man, he wanted to touch him and feel him and to have those lips on his body. And then he saw how perfect he was, the strength and grace and power that was his, and he remembered all over again about his leg.

He ducked his head and blindly pushed his way back to the door—he didn't know how it was he had come so far into the room—and out into the damp night air.

Chapter Three

The next day, Captain Fanshawe did not put Captain Courtenay to shame by the time of his arrival at Horse Guards. In fact, Captain Fanshawe had arrived mere minutes before Captain Courtenay, and he still had not done so much as look at the papers on his desk. His head pounded and his stomach was delicate from the amount of brandy he had drunk on his return to his chambers last night in a desperate attempt to forget the entire humiliating experience. He had also sought to drive from his mind the images that haunted him, of men kissing one another, their hands roaming under one another's clothes, and those grey eyes that had seen everything. But no matter how hard he tried, he was unable to forget.

He groaned and dropped his head into his hands.

"Another thrilling night on the marriage mart at Almack's?" Courtenay's mocking tones announced his arrival. "I cannot conceive how you bear such excitement."

Hugh rubbed his hands over his face and looked up.

"Good God." Courtenay stared at him. "Do you mean to tell me that Captain Dutiful was in his cups last night? And I was not invited to observe such a spectacle? I am cut to the quick, Fanshawe." He put a hand to his wounded heart.

Hugh simply shook his head dismissively, waited for the resulting nausea to subside, then bent his attention to the papers that awaited him.

Working through them for the next few hours gave him a chance to recover somewhat from his delicate state, and by the time a knock sounded at the door, he was almost restored. That state of affairs lasted until he glanced up, and then he clambered swiftly to his feet and stood at attention, sure he swayed slightly as the blood rushed from his brain to leave him light-headed, his heart pounding so hard it threatened to burst from his chest.

There was an officer standing in the doorway. An officer with a brow that was high and noble, a jawline that was clean and strong, lips that were neither too full nor ungenerous and penetrating grey eyes. The officer returned Hugh's regard for a moment, with a suggestion of amusement in his face, and then sauntered into the office. As his gaze left Hugh to survey Courtenay, Hugh had the opportunity to take in the full effect of his powerful yet lean body, shown to advantage by the uniform he wore. The dark green uniform of the Rifles. Hugh swallowed and wondered if he had poisoned himself with too much brandy and would soon be dead after such vivid fever dreams.

"Colonel Theo Lindsay, 95th Rifles," he said. "No need to stand, gentlemen. I am merely seeking a diversion while I await the Adjutant General's pleasure."

Hugh swallowed again and blindly felt his way back down into his seat, unable to take his eyes from the colonel. Surely it could not be... Surely he must be mistaken, his thoughts of the man from last night meaning he saw similarities where there could be none. This was Sophia's partner from the ball, and that was what had caused the jolt of recognition. Yet something deep inside him knew otherwise.

"Captain, are you quite well?"

"Thank you, sir, I am." He tore his eyes from Colonel Lindsay's face and fixed them on the papers in front of him. He was in no doubt that the colour in his cheeks was fluctuating between white as bone to a pink that would put Miss Williams to shame.

"Captain Fanshawe dipped a little too deep last night," Courtenay put in, and Hugh had never thought he would have reason to be grateful to Courtenay. "Captain Francis Courtenay, 52nd Foot, at your service, sir."

"Indeed."

Hugh dared to look up again and found Colonel Lindsay surveying them both with an air of faint boredom. "Tell me, gentlemen, as one only recently returned to these shores, where might one expect to pass an enjoyable evening these days?"

Hugh looked down again. He knew the colonel could not be teasing Hugh by making an elliptical reference to the previous night. The very thought of it, however, meant he could not hold the colonel's gaze.

Thankfully, Courtenay saved the day. Talking had always been more to his liking than working, and with a senior office initiating conversation, what could he do but fling himself wholeheartedly into it? Colonel Lindsay moved across the room to Courtenay's desk and propped a hip on it as he toyed with Courtenay's quill, listening to the reeling off of a list of new gambling hells, the best places to attend prizefights these days, the latest opera dancers in Covent Garden and so on. In a burst of amity, they arranged for Lindsay to accompany Courtenay to the most recent exclusive hell to have opened, where Lindsay was assured that play was for those with deep pockets and no rackety types were allowed through the hallowed portals.

"What of you, Captain Fanshawe? Will you join us?"

Hugh looked up from where he had been pretending to study his paperwork and found Colonel Lindsay watching him with friendly invitation in his face.

Courtenay's crack of laughter split the air before Hugh could respond. "Captain Fanshawe spends his every evening on his mama's leading string," he informed Colonel Lindsay. "Indeed, I have no idea how he contrived to slip free long enough to fight overseas, unless his brother agreed to wet-nurse him."

Hugh sat rigid for an instant, scarcely able to credit his ears. He and Courtenay had never been friends and he knew the man had a tart tongue, yet he had never realised the depth of scorn that informed his opinion of Hugh. And the reason why they had not become friends, despite sharing this office for four months, was laid bare in Courtenay's words—he understood neither obligation, nor duty, nor kindness to one's widowed parent who sought only diversion from her single state.

"I regret I have another commitment this evening, sir," he said to Lindsay. "Another time, perhaps."

"When the seas have run dry," Courtenay muttered, and when Hugh looked sharply at him, he raised his eyebrows in response. "You know it to be true," he said, then looked back to Lindsay and shrugged slightly, as if to underline how difficult a time he had sharing an office with such a dull bore.

"I shall hold you to that, Fanshawe," Lindsay said, and it took Hugh an instant to remember to what he was to be held.

"Ten o'clock, then," Lindsay said to Courtenay in parting. He nodded to them both, and retreated as casually and in as unhurried a manner as he had arrived.

Hugh still felt unsettled on returning to his lodgings, to such an extent that he seized thankfully upon the missive from his mother that reminded him his presence was expected for a small dinner party that evening. Even that would be better than facing an evening with nothing to distract him from his thoughts.

He was sure in his own mind, as sure as he could be after partaking as heavily as he had, that it had been Lindsay he had seen last night. He knew Lindsay had marked his presence and had subjected him to enough scrutiny that there could be no doubt of him recognising Hugh again. Yet what could Hugh do?

He could scarcely approach the man and fall into conversation about the molly house they had both visited. It left him uneasy not to address the issue, however, because each time he thought of Lindsay, Hugh wondered if his presence at such a place might yet be betrayed. Hugh's peace of mind wasn't helped by thoughts of Lindsay's figure—the strength that was so evident in his shoulders and the long lines of his powerful thighs in close-fitting green pantaloons.

Requiring a diversion from such thoughts, he took some time choosing his outfit that evening, to the great delight of his valet who seemed to take it as a personal insult that Hugh preferred simple clothes when not in uniform. As Murray dressed him, he managed to convey to Hugh in no uncertain terms that if only Hugh could rid himself of his deplorable habit of patronising Scott rather than Weston for his coats, he might even meet with his valet's approval. Despite the obligatory lugubriousness that descended upon Murray's features when he brushed his gloved hands across Hugh's shoulders and the entirely inferior coat, he couldn't hide the air of satisfaction that suffused him that at last his master was almost doing him credit. Hugh thought perhaps he should indulge Murray a little more in his choice of dress, because it appeared not to take much to make him happy and he was a most excellent man who ran Hugh's modest household in precisely the way that made Hugh comfortable. Going to Weston for his coats was an indulgence too far, however.

Hugh arrived at the house in Half Moon Street to find that his mother's idea of what constituted a small party was somewhat at variance with his. He put the best face on it he could and took the opportunity shortly after his arrival to snatch a few quiet words with Sophia. At least, that was his intention, but he found her deep in conversation with Miss Williams. As he approached, he was almost sure he could see Sophia's clever touches in Miss Williams' appearance tonight, for while her hair was still *à la mode*, it was more flattering in style, and the flowers twisted into it were cream rather than white, lending her hair a softer hue.

"C-captain Fanshawe," Miss Williams greeted him, her cheeks growing rosier by the instant.

"Your servant, Miss Williams," he returned, and wondered briefly at the quizzical look he received from Sophia. "Were you able to resolve satisfactorily your puzzle about shops?"

"Oh yes," Miss Williams said, hands clasped together earnestly. "Thanks to your kindness and to Sophia, who has been *so* helpful."

"I'm delighted to hear it," Hugh said, and wondered just how he was going to speak to Sophia without Miss Williams hanging on their every word.

"Lavinia," Sophia said, "would you think it terribly remiss of me to speak for an instant to Hugh about the letter we had today from James?"

"Oh!" Miss Williams said, and the colour which had begun to fade blazed up again in her face. "I'm sorry—I did not—of course. I shall go and speak to Lady Melksham, for she was so very gracious earlier."

Hugh looked apologetically at Sophia once they were alone. "Are you very out of sorts with me for introducing you?" Had he realised just how socially hobbled Miss Williams was, he would not have imposed her on Sophia.

"Not at all," she returned strongly. "She is the sweetest thing, and she is not usually so easily overset. I cannot think why she should be so tonight."

Hugh was fairly certain that Sophia's words were loaded, accompanied as they were by a particularly speaking look, but he did not have the interest in Miss Williams to pursue Sophia's meaning.

"What does James have to say?" he asked.

Sophia looked confused for an instant, then she put her hand on Hugh's arm. "Oh, there is no letter. Forgive me for being so scheming, but I thought you wanted to speak to me and could not do so with Lavinia here."

"It's nothing of import," he said swiftly, not wishing Sophia to refine too much upon his subject matter, and also wondering just when Sophia had developed Emily's ability of being able to see into his mind. "I merely wished to know how you are. Did you enjoy yesterday evening?"

"Very much," she said. "There were quite a number present, and such dancing, Hugh—you should have seen the tangle that resulted when Thomas Ivory stood upon Isabella's gown and it tore. It brought the entire room to a standstill."

"And did you fall upon the side of *clumsy oaf* or *poor unfortunate*?" he teased, because Sophia's heart was very tender.

"It might have happened to anyone," she scolded him, then added after a moment's reflection, "although he is perhaps a little more prone to it than most."

"Did you stand up with anyone in particular?"

Her brow creased slightly. "Sir Ralph was not present." Perhaps she heard the clear dejection in her voice because she rushed on to add, "And of course the Marquess would not attend such a gathering. Not," she confided in a lower voice, leaning in towards him, "that I am quite so enamoured of him as Mama appears to be."

No, that would be difficult indeed. He was, however, pleased to learn of the wretched Stanton's continuing absence and only hoped it was due to him having found an heiress to court rather than it being a game he was playing with Sophia to ensure she was all the more receptive when he once more appeared in her orbit.

There was nothing Hugh could do about that at the moment, so he changed the subject to the heart of what he wanted to know. "Will you guess who came into my office today?"

"Good heavens, Hugh—not The Most Honourable The Marquess of Wellington?"

"Brat," he shot at her, as she clasped her hands in excitement and her face lit with pretended anticipation and delight. "You know as well as I that Wellington refuses to return to England for as long as we are at war."

"Well, I don't know who else might have you so excited, brother dearest. Do tell."

Excited? That was an interesting word for the mixture of emotions that thoughts of Colonel Lindsay raised in Hugh's breast. "Your partner from the Fitzroys' ball, Colonel Lindsay of the 95th Rifles."

"Oh," Sophia said blankly. Hugh's great revelation had evidently proved hugely anticlimactic.

"He had business at Horse Guards," Hugh laboured on determinedly. "Did he happen to mention what brought him back to England when you spoke to him?" Because if Hugh knew that, he might gain some indication as to how long he would be in London.

She shook her head, chestnut curls bouncing.

"Lindsay, you say?" He had not noticed his mother's approach until she interrupted his and Sophia's exchange. "He's younger son to the Earl of Badbury. A good fortune too, I believe, from his uncle, Winslow." It seemed the content of their conversation was suddenly borne in upon her because sudden eagerness and calculation showed in her face. "You stood up with him, Sophia?"

"For one dance, and he was merely being polite," she said, and her lack of interest in Lindsay could scarcely be more plain.

Hugh could not help but wonder at it. What would possess a lady to favour a ramshackle fool like Stanton, who modelled himself after one of Lord Byron's romantic heroes, above the address and figure of a man such as Lindsay?

"I believe Colonel Lindsay is only here briefly, for he mentioned business with the Adjutant General," he said, determined to steer his mother away from any further thoughts about Lindsay. "Now, Mama, tell me just how it is you contrive to look more beautiful each time I see you?"

"Flatterer." She tapped him sharply on the arm with her fan, although a smile graced her lips. "Come with me, I wish to introduce you to Lord Maplethorpe. His youngest is in the Peninsula and he wishes to ask you about the situation over there."

As Hugh obediently accompanied her across the room, he hoped he had nipped his mother's interest in Colonel Lindsay in the bud. The thought of Lindsay marrying Sophia left him feeling somehow hollow inside.

Chapter Four

The following day, Hugh devoted himself to his work. Even though he couldn't see how his contribution was helping achieve victory over Boney, he had to believe it was useful in some way, if only to those officers who had requested leave.

Courtenay did not appear until late in the day. When he did so he was pale, his eyes were bloodshot and his hair looked as though it had not recently known the attentions of a comb.

"Dear God," he exclaimed dramatically, staggering over to his desk and falling gracefully into the chair there. "What *is* it about the Rifles? Never go drinking with a rifleman, Fanshawe. It ain't worth the pain afterwards."

Hugh felt no particular friendship for Courtenay after yesterday's revelation of his true feelings, so he held his silence. It didn't deter Courtenay from continuing to make his condition known, for he sighed exaggeratedly a great many times before he dropped his head down onto his desk, his groan muffled somewhat by the piles of papers on which his face rested. Hugh continued to work, scratching careful notations into the regimental books in front of him and compiling memoranda for Colonel Dalrymple as requested, and trying his best not to be distracted by Courtenay's continued sprawl across his desk or the snores that ultimately emanated from his outstretched figure.

When Hugh rose to his feet at the end of the day, leaving a neat stack of new paperwork on the corner of his desk, he hesitated for an instant over whether or not to alert Courtenay to the onset of evening. He decided to leave him to continue sleeping. His decision may have been influenced the smallest part by Courtenay's attitude the previous day. It was most certainly *not* due to Hugh's envy that Courtenay had evidently enjoyed a long and pleasurable evening with Colonel Lindsay. That thought didn't even cross his mind as he put on his greatcoat and headed back to his lodgings, and it did not stay with him as he dressed for yet another ball. His attention was entirely upon his outfit, as his valet would vouch.

When he arrived at Half Moon Street, Lady Fanshawe greeted him with unusual enthusiasm. "You look quite the thing tonight, Hugh, even if you are not in regimentals."

Startled, he glanced in the looking glass above the fireplace, to find that Murray had dressed him in a coat of blue superfine with gold buttons that shone in the light, a white silk waistcoat and satin knee breeches, and had evidently persuaded him while his mind was elsewhere to tie his neckcloth in the Mathematical style.

"Hugh!" Sophia greeted him as she came into the room. "Have you seen my new gown? It is apple-blossom crape, and just see how the beads and drops are arranged *á la militaire*. It is quite as splendid as your regimentals but much prettier. I have decided it is one of my very favourites."

Hugh found it difficult to tell the difference between this particular gown and any of the other ball dresses Sophia wore, but he knew better than to volunteer that information. He admired it suitably, making her smile. Then she turned her gaze upon him.

"You look bang up to the mark tonight," she said, and laughed at his disapproval. "I know I shouldn't use such an expression, but it's true. Is there a particular lady whose eye you wish to catch?"

Hugh spread his hands out in a plea. "Can a fellow not dress to gladden the heart of his valet once in a while without being assailed for it?"

"Evidently not," Sophia said. "Come, we mustn't be late."

Which must mean she was expecting Stanton's presence tonight. Hugh was suddenly glad he had agreed to accompany them.

The ballroom at the Trents' townhouse was crowded, hot and noisy. Hugh did not like his chances of keeping a close eye upon Sophia in such circumstances and had to trust to his mother's experience of chaperoning, as well as to Sophia's own good sense. He didn't want to believe she would ever do anything improper, but her incomprehensible fondness for Stanton might allow him to persuade her into something that she would in no other situation consider. He set no store in the power of Miss Williams to dissuade her; he had already greeted that young lady this evening, to be met with more blushes and stammers that had trailed off into such a tangle of half-formed sentences that he had been forced to hold forth on the subject of the weather at excruciating length in order to give her time to recover her countenance. He had finally been able to retreat when their hostess approached with a fair-haired young man whose blush equalled Miss Williams' own and who appeared desirous of making her acquaintance.

As Hugh circled the room, he searched for Stanton. He was, at least, always easy to see—he was far too emotionally tortured to bother with such mundane things as styling his hair, and his rebellion against society's strictures found expression in waistcoats of a most alarming range of colours and patterns.

Hugh's thoughts about Stanton had driven other matters from his mind and so it took him a while to realise he was not imagining the flash of dark green uniform with silver buttons and red silk sash that he glimpsed from the corner of his eye. Turning on the spot, he saw the familiar figure that could only belong to Colonel Theo Lindsay making his bow to Emily, who was regarding him with distinct approval in her face. She laughed at something Lindsay said, and Hugh was familiar enough with her to know it was not mere politeness but true amusement. Something twinged within his breast, and he turned his attention to searching for Stanton once more.

Sometime later, he completed his circuit of the ballroom, only to observe that somehow he had missed his quarry, for Sophia was standing up with the cursed Stanton. Emily and Lindsay also formed part of the set. Hugh leaned back against the wall and watched. If there was the suspicion of a glower upon his face, it was to do with Stanton's temerity, nothing more. He was quite obviously charming Sophia with his attentions, and even Hugh had to admit that he was a very handsome fellow, if one could overlook his reprehensible character and sartorial solecisms.

Hugh's brow lowered further once the dance had finished because Emily, of all people, was presenting Lindsay to Sophia, and she was standing up with him for the next dance. Even seeing Stanton necessarily prevented from further contact with Sophia in such a way did not calm him. When he realised that supper was to follow the dance, meaning Lindsay would accompany Sophia, it was all he could do not to grind his teeth. It was scant comfort to see that no matter how Sophia's head might have been turned by Stanton, she was still behaving properly, turning all her attention on her current partner and smiling prettily at whatever he was saying. Hugh wondered just what it was Lindsay said that caused each of his partners such pleasure in his company.

"Really, Hugh—have you the gout?"

He turned to find Emily smiling at him.

"You look positively saturnine. If I did not know you better, I might find myself frightened to approach such a forbidding figure."

He could not help but smile at her exaggerations. "Forgive me," he said. "I was watching Stanton with Sophia. It's clear he still harbours intentions towards her. I must speak with her, I suppose."

"Hugh, no!" The very real alarm in her voice took him by surprise. "Do not even *think* of doing such a thing—it would be disastrous."

"How so?"

"Can you not see that a romance forbidden by her straitlaced brother would make the illicit union only more attractive, for it would cast them in the part of star-crossed lovers?"

"No," he said bluntly. "That is nonsensical."

Emily sighed, but there was laughter in her eyes. "Dearest Hugh," she said. "That is why you must not, on any account, speak to her—you have not the least understanding of the emotions of a young lady who considers herself in love. Leave it to me. I shall make sure to depress her good opinion of him with withering comment at suitable opportunities, and she will soon come to see that what appears to be romantic in him is in fact ridiculous. I have every faith in your sister's good sense."

"As have I," Hugh returned swiftly. Although he did not share the thought with Emily, he also had faith in Stanton's inability to remain constant in his objective if it was not easily achieved. No matter what Emily believed, he had enough understanding of young ladies' hearts to know that even the most hardened of rakes could scarcely woo two at once and expect them both to remain receptive to his advances.

"In any case, she appears to be quite charmed by her current partner, so it is entirely possible that Stanton will be sent packing."

Hugh eyed Sophia and Lindsay with misgiving. It was true she was smiling up at him, the resulting dimples in her cheeks making her look particularly fetching. "You think Lindsay has an interest there?"

Emily's breath caught and she choked slightly.

"May I fetch you a glass of orgeat?" Hugh asked, concerned, as she fought to breathe.

"I'm quite all right, thank you, Hugh," she said, once she was able. "I think the good colonel's interest does not lie with Sophia."

Hugh felt insensibly reassured. His good humour continued despite the fact he had to accompany the Dowager Countess of Royston to supper, during which he was subjected to a litany of the achievements of her son, Harry, against Napoleon. Apparently he had no need of Wellington nor the rest of the army to achieve victory. Hugh had not had the pleasure of encountering the gentleman in question—he determined to ask James next time they were together whether the man was as insufferable and boastful a prig as his mother made him sound or if it was just the ravings of a fond mama that did him no favours. At least not having to contribute to the conversation made it easy for him to keep a casual eye upon Sophia, just in case Stanton broke with all propriety and attempted to approach her during supper. She appeared to be talking intently with Colonel Lindsay, and from all he could tell they were enjoying a most convivial time.

After supper, he retired to the card room. Having enjoyed a game of whist with some gentlemen also seeking sanctuary from the dancing, he took his leave of them and headed back towards the ballroom to check that all was well with Sophia and to see who else might be about. On his way from the card room he was taken by surprise to see Colonel Lindsay standing in the doorway, his grey eyes fixed on Hugh's limping progress towards him.

Before Hugh could greet him, Lindsay spoke. "I heard from Courtenay that you were not one for deep play, Fanshawe."

"That, sir, is why I restrict my gaming to assemblies and balls."

Lindsay's lips twitched slightly. "I am seeking refuge from matchmaking mamas who are desirous I stand up for every dance," he confessed. "Will you assist me?"

"There's a conservatory at the end of the hall," Hugh said, never expecting to have a reason to be thankful for the number of entertainments his mother had induced him to attend in this very house. He made his way along the hall to show Lindsay. "It should be cooler there too."

"Thank God for that," Lindsay said, and no sooner was he through the doors of the unoccupied conservatory than he undid the top buttons of his uniform coat. "That's better," he said, seating himself on the long sofa that was against one wall. "How do you survive these things every night?"

He was evidently expecting Hugh to join him in conversation rather than retire once he'd shown him the conservatory, so Hugh sat down on the other end of the sofa from Lindsay. "One becomes inured," he said. "It helps that I'm no longer in demand on the marriage mart."

"You must tell me how you have managed that particular feat. I had not thought it possible without losing one's entire fortune or offending against all propriety, and I do not believe you capable of either of those things."

"It is on account of my leg."

"I see." Lindsay's tone was matter-of-fact, filled with neither pity nor embarrassment, unlike most. "Does it bother you much?"

"It is, as my brother James was at pains to explain to me, merely a minor inconvenience." Hugh smiled slightly at the memory. It was either that or weep. "I believe he was attempting to cheer me."

"Yes, I can see how that would have worked," Lindsay said, his voice as dry as the Spanish central plains. "Major James Fanshawe is on Wellington's Staff, is he not?"

"He is, although he is wishful for leave because he means to marry Miss Drury."

"So many good men rushing into matrimony," Lindsay mused. "It's enough to make one despair." He paused for a moment, then turned his head and looked directly at Hugh, his eyes compelling. "That reminds me of something I wished to raise with you. Horse Guards was not the first time we met."

Despite the sudden clench of his stomach, Hugh held Lindsay's gaze steadily, for he was not a coward. "It was not," he said quietly. "I saw you in the Strand."

"Would I be correct in thinking that you do not often frequent such establishments?"

Heat rose in Hugh's cheeks for an instant. He didn't know why it should matter to him that Lindsay thought him a dull fellow, but he could not lie. "That was the first time."

"A word of advice, Fanshawe, if I might presume—there are risks associated with such places. If you wish, I could make introductions elsewhere for you."

Discomfited, Hugh knew neither where to look nor what to say.

"Such houses are more for working men, and there are other places where you would be safe, that is all I mean," Lindsay said.

He waited for an instant, and when Hugh remained tongue-tied, he changed the subject as if the previous exchange had never happened. "Tell me, what must one do to gain audience with the Adjutant General? Every day I am told to report, and every day I am told he is far too busy for nuisances such as I. If this keeps up, I will return to Portugal to find the Rifles have left without me, for they're to march to Alcántara in three weeks' time."

"Is there nobody else to whom you can discharge your business?" Hugh asked.

"It would appear not," Lindsay said. "So I suppose I must prepare myself for continued idleness among the good people of the *ton*. When I bought my commission, I didn't expect that my battles would be fought against matchmaking mamas in the ballrooms of London."

Hugh grinned. "I feel sure you are too experienced a campaigner to be caught by their stratagems."

Lindsay stretched his legs—his long, powerful legs—in front of him. "I dare say," he said carelessly, "but there are times it feels as if I am engaged upon a forlorn hope."

Having seen his own mama at work when it came to trying to arrange the most advantageous marriage possible for her daughter, Hugh could not gainsay the similarity. "In which case, we will be sure to mourn your inevitable demise and honour your memory suitably."

Lindsay laughed suddenly. It transformed his face, making him appear open and happy and, if such a thing were possible, even more handsome. "You should have more sympathy, Fanshawe—being overlooked by the matchmaking mamas does not render you entirely free from the prospect of being laid to siege," he said. "I know of at least two ladies tonight who appeared quite cast down whenever you were out of their sight."

Hugh stared at Lindsay. He couldn't imagine why he would say such a thing, unless it was to mock Hugh. Lindsay looked at him, and Hugh had the sense he had experienced in the molly house, that Lindsay was seeing to the very depths of him. It was an uncomfortable feeling, but one he was somehow reluctant to lose.

"You really have no idea, do you?" Lindsay said, and he sounded surprised.

The conservatory doors opened abruptly, and the sound of chatter and music swirled in, along with three young gentlemen who appeared to have dipped a little too deep.

"Back to it, I suppose," Lindsay said, and buttoned his uniform coat. "Tell me, Fanshawe, will you dine with me tomorrow at The Clarendon?"

"I should be delighted, sir," Hugh said as he levered himself clumsily to his feet, because it was both the polite answer and the truth. Although, as he parted ways with Lindsay on regaining the heat and noise of the ballroom and watched the man walking away, he was not entirely sure it had been sensible of him to accept the invitation.

He decided he must put from his mind any thoughts about how Lindsay looked and simply enjoy the company of another military man, free from the stifling atmosphere of balls and assemblies. That might not quiet the feelings that Theo Lindsay stirred in him, but it would be enough. It would have to be.

Chapter Five

Hugh almost failed to recognise Lindsay the next evening when he arrived at the hotel, for the man was out of uniform. The dark green of the Rifles uniform suited him so well it might have been designed especially for him, but the clothes he wore instead also displayed his figure to full advantage. His elegant plum tailcoat, which looked as though it were moulded to his body, showed the breadth of his shoulders, and his skintight fawn pantaloons hid nothing of the muscle in his thighs. Nor did they hide anything else, for that matter. Hugh found it a struggle to keep his eyes on Lindsay's face as they greeted one another.

Once they had taken their seats and Lindsay had explained his reasoning in quite apologetic tones for inviting Hugh to a hotel instead of his club, Hugh found he was responding to the friendliness in Lindsay's eyes and that the perfection of his body was becoming easier to—well, not forget, precisely, but put to the back of his mind. It appeared that Lindsay's intention had been to enjoy a more private conversation with Hugh than a club would have allowed, and his choice of hotel assured them of a meal better than they would have enjoyed in any of the clubs except for Watier's.

"Although even the dinners there do not entirely make up for the company," Lindsay admitted.

"I wouldn't expect you to be a member of such a place," Hugh confessed, emboldened by Lindsay's frankness.

"You do not see me as one of the dandy set? Fanshawe, I am quite cast down by your judgment upon my sartorial shortcomings." But Lindsay's eyes were full of laughter, and Hugh knew he had not offended, despite his somewhat infelicitous words. "I know of the club's reputation, but sometimes even the most intelligent of men hides himself behind affectation or an assumed manner, for amusement or some other purpose. It does not do to judge by first impressions."

Hugh merely nodded, for he had never been good at summing up people swiftly in the way Emily seemed so easily to do. And then he thought of Stanton, whom he had pegged in an instant.

"I'm sure you're right," he said, "although occasionally a first impression is the right one and to be forced to further the acquaintance is punishment indeed."

"True," Lindsay said, then he leaned across the table towards Hugh. "I would hope, however, you do not count me among the unfortunate fellows whose acquaintance you would choose not to pursue."

The laughter in his face was mixed with something that looked like invitation, and Hugh felt his cheeks warm slightly, for surely Colonel Lindsay could not be flirting with him. Thankfully, before his inability to think of a reply became obvious, they were interrupted by the waiter bringing their first course. Lindsay's choice of venue was more than justified, for they supped on a delightful jardinière soup, removed with turbot and trout à la genevoise.

As they awaited their entrées, Hugh asked Lindsay a question to which he almost dreaded the answer. "Have you had any success with the Adjutant General?"

"If by success you mean have I grown more intimately familiar with his antechamber, then yes, I suppose I have."

Hugh tried not to show his pleasure at Lindsay's response. "You would always be welcome in our office should you desire a change of scene. So long as you did not come bearing drink, for I think Courtenay has not yet recovered from your evening together."

Lindsay snorted. "Light Bobs. They deserve their name."

Hugh grinned, then took the opportunity of making mockery of an obviously inferior regiment to ask something he had wondered about. "What led you to join the Rifles?"

Lindsay sat back in his chair. "I find the Rifles intriguing—they are far more flexible, more *interesting* than the long-established regiments." He smiled suddenly, one which showed a lot of teeth. "I also happen to like their Baker rifles. So much more accurate than the Brown Bess."

The waiter brought more dishes at that point, and conversation was briefly suspended while they were served. Once the man had retreated, his shoes silent on the thick carpet, Lindsay continued.

"Of course, my going into the Rifles caused my father practically to disown me, breaking with family tradition in such a way. I take it you did not have that problem, following your brother as you did into the 7th Foot?"

"My only difficulty was my mother's determination that I should enter the church instead of buying a commission."

"What a waste that would have been," Lindsay declared, as he speared a piece of quail with his fork.

Hugh was not sure of Lindsay's meaning, so he concentrated on the food on his own plate.

"Perhaps I will take you up on your offer to cool my heels in your office rather than the antechamber," Lindsay continued. "At least there I will not have to overhear the heated discussions about Wellington's fitness to command."

Hugh's head shot up, and he fixed his eyes on Lindsay's face. He knew there were disagreements between Horse Guards and Wellington, but had no idea they were that serious.

"Surely they can't mean that," he protested. "He has secured so many victories, and it is only a matter of time before he has the French on the run for good."

"But look at the time it has taken him and the men he has lost. Not to mention what it has cost the country." Lindsay's smile was mocking. "And when I say do not mention it, I mean do *not* mention it, for they do not give a fig about the men lost, but pretending they do sounds so much better than protesting at the expense of the campaign."

"Do they think anyone else could have done better?" Hugh asked, anger licking up in him.

"As to that..." Lindsay put down his cutlery and leaned back in his chair as he gave it careful consideration. "Given the officers they keep foisting upon Wellington, I suggest the answer to your question is yes. Would you believe, when he complained about Erskine being a madman, he was told simply that during his lucid intervals, he was uncommonly clever? And only yesterday, I thought the Military Secretary was about to go off in an apoplexy on receipt of one of Wellington's letters. When he read out choice parts of it to the Adjutant General, which I could hear perfectly well even from where I was sitting because he was so incensed, I could understand why—Wellington hoped, among other things, that when the enemy reads the names of his generals, he trembles as much as Wellington did."

Hugh couldn't hold back his laughter. It encouraged Lindsay, who observed him with eyes that danced with humour. "It is, I think, the iciness with which Wellington delivers his setdowns that has the administration so incensed. Oh God, Fanshawe, you should have heard him when Gordon lost the supply column—not a heated word from him, despite the fact he had been out there personally quartering the countryside in search of his truants, but instead the most terrifyingly cold and devastating reproach I have ever heard. And when in the course of his search he encountered the officer in charge of baggage, who confessed to him that he had lost the baggage, Wellington didn't fly off into a temper but instead answered him, 'Well, I can't be surprised, for I cannot find my army'."

Hugh's laughter was as much at Lindsay's great delight in the outrageous tales as it was at their content. But then the seriousness of the underlying problem struck him, and it was exactly what he had thought, about men being promoted by seniority rather than ability.

"This is precisely—" He stopped suddenly, for he recollected himself. It was one thing to speak of his fears to James in the morning room in Half Moon Street where they could not be overheard; another entirely to volunteer them to a man who was, he must remember, no more than an acquaintance, no matter how comfortable his company, and who was moreover a senior officer. As was James, of course, but they were brothers first and foremost.

Lindsay's eyebrows rose as he waited for Hugh to continue.

"I suppose it is difficult with the newspapers making criticisms and the people not understanding the exigencies of the campaign," Hugh supplied swiftly. "Horse Guards must wish to ensure that everything is done properly. Though I wish the newspapers would write of what Wellington has done to look after his men, the lighter cooking kettles he has provided, the tents and the hospitals he has instituted. Perhaps then people would not be so swift to criticise."

"Perhaps," Lindsay said, "though I think you are too kind in your estimation." He picked up his glass and sipped at the extremely good hock with which they had been furnished. "I daresay all will be over soon, anyway—with the key promotions that are being made in the 29th Foot, it seems to me likely that Wellington will be opening a second front in Holland."

It sounded too good to be true that the war might finally be over, but for a short while Hugh let himself believe it, and he smiled. "At least then the *ton* will be swamped with returning officers in their regimentals—which, my mother assures me, are quite the ladies' favourites—and you may find yourself run to earth less often."

"I hope to God you're right," Lindsay said. "I swear, the forced march to Talavera was a breeze compared to standing up for so many dances with so many very young ladies last night. I was beginning to think I must somehow contrive to lose my fortune and see if my father will oblige me by casting me off."

"I think that may be a little excessive," Hugh pointed out. "Perhaps simply setting up a flirt might secure the same outcome."

"As you have done?"

Hugh stared at him in confusion.

"Lady Emily d'Arcourt," Lindsay elucidated.

Hugh stiffened slightly, for Lindsay was mistaken and he did not appreciate hearing Emily's name bandied about like that, even in private conversation. "She was sister to my dear friend, Lord Robert Trevelyan," he said reprovingly. "He was killed at Talavera."

"I understand she has been widowed," Lindsay said. "Her husband was a Frenchman."

"Yes." Hugh was not going to discuss Emily, even with Lindsay.

"No need to be so fierce, my dear Fanshawe—I have no designs upon Lady Emily."

As the waiter returned, Lindsay steered conversation into general conversation about shared experiences in Portugal and Spain. By the time the night grew old, Hugh had decided that not only was Theo Lindsay the most attractive man he had ever laid eyes on, but the most convivial companion also. He struggled not to be disappointed when Lindsay finally stretched in his seat and concluded that they had best call it a night.

"Because I intend to report bright and early tomorrow morning at Horse Guards. Perhaps if I can catch him on the way *in* to his office, I might have more success."

Hugh was not entirely convinced—he knew how busy a man the Adjutant General was, and a colonel from the Rifles would not really register on his priorities. On the other hand, he was reasonably certain that whatever Colonel Theo Lindsay wanted, he would get, so he would not like to wager on the outcome.

They parted on the steps of the hotel. As Hugh wound his slightly meandering way home—the wine and port had been excellent, after all, necessitating several glasses to be enjoyed—he found he was smiling broadly. Not least because Lindsay had said they should do this again before much longer, if Hugh were not too busy in the ballrooms of London. Hugh had instantly decried such a thing, privately determining to cancel any and every engagement his mother had made on his behalf so he might be guaranteed to be available whenever Lindsay wished to spend another evening with him.

Chapter Six

April announced its arrival with a succession of cold and damp days. As he broke off from his work to watch the Life Guards drill on the parade ground, Hugh was thankful that he was safely behind a window, with a warm fire burning in the grate. He had not seen Lindsay since their dinner. After a couple of evenings when he had returned home eagerly, wanting to see if an invitation awaited him in his lodgings, he had regained his equilibrium. No matter how polite he'd been, the man would scarcely wish to spend all his time with someone like Hugh.

He hadn't realised he'd sighed until Courtenay's voice cut across him. "God's sake, Fanshawe, when did you become a repining ninny? More importantly, for whom are you threatening to enter a decline brought about by a broken heart? I had thought you to be entirely ineligible these days, damaged goods, unlikely to be snapped up by any lady of looks or fortune."

"My apologies for disturbing you," Hugh responded stiffly. "I shall endeavour not to do so again."

"Oh for God's sake, Fanshawe, there's no need to be so full of starch. We're friends, after all, are we not? Can you not take a little ribbing? Now tell me—I know all the signs of a man in love, and your every feeling is always writ large upon your face. Who is she?"

"You're mistaken, Courtenay," Hugh said, turning away from the window and looking at him, attempting civility. "I merely detest the weather and am wishful for the sun."

"If you say so." But Courtenay's eyes were sharp, and Hugh felt uncomfortable beneath his scrutiny. "So perhaps you will accompany Lindsay and me to the opera tonight, for there is a bevy of new dancers, all of whom are most welcoming and amenable. There is one in particular, a dark-haired beauty, Arabella, whom I can fully recommend—she is most talented."

"Thank you, but I am otherwise engaged tonight," Hugh said with a smile. A smile that threatened to hurt his face with the effort it had taken to manufacture. "Only remember the dangers of drinking with the Rifles," he went on, in a laborious attempt at levity, for he did not wish to reject entirely Courtenay's idea of an olive branch. "I don't wish to leave you to spend the night here again."

"I don't think the desks were designed for comfort," Courtenay agreed. "Now, have you the records for the Coldstream or must I go in fear and trembling to the ferocious Colonel Badham?"

"I have them here somewhere." Hugh extracted them from the pile on his desk and attempted to lose himself in his work as Courtenay flicked through the records, papers rustling as he did so.

So Lindsay was engaged with Courtenay again tonight? He should not be surprised—Courtenay's darting mind and lively personality, always ready with an amusing quip, left Hugh feeling like a lumbering clumsy ox. Lindsay had only been being polite when he had suggested meeting Hugh again for another evening. Hugh knew he had no reason for the disappointment that sat heavy in his stomach, and he tried to lose it by burying himself in work.

On returning to his lodgings that evening, he found a missive from his mother inviting him to a family dinner. He was glad to send back an acceptance, knowing such an evening would distract him from other matters. When he arrived at Half Moon Street, he was even more glad he had accepted, for when Matthews announced him, he found James standing in the middle of the drawing room. He looked resplendent in his scarlet coat and gleaming boots, and there was a wide smile on his handsome face.

"Hugh!" James crossed the room to him in a few swift paces and took him into a hug that pulled Hugh quite off balance. "How are you, brother?"

Hugh returned the hug, delighted and surprised. "Well, I thank you. How are things over there? And how have you managed to come home on leave without me knowing of it?"

"It is one of the advantages of being on Wellington's Personal Staff," James said smugly. "He orders us as he pleases, not as the stuffed shirts at Horse Guards insist."

Their mama chimed in at that point, wishing to continue telling James all about Sophia's success in the eyes of the *ton*—almost as successful as her own first season, in fact. This subject, along with discussion of James's upcoming nuptials and George's burgeoning political career, which meant he was far too busy with parliament business to join them tonight, dominated the conversation throughout dinner.

Finally the ladies and the servants withdrew, leaving James and Hugh to enjoy their port in peace.

"How goes it, James?" Hugh asked, at last able to turn to military matters.

James was silent for a while, causing Hugh's heart to beat faster. Such stillness from James, of all people, could not mean anything good.

"There are problems with the Portuguese—their government says they have not the money to pay the army. Wellington insists the money is there, but the will is not. And meanwhile the people grow to hate us, robbing and killing British soldiers with apparent impunity. As for the Spaniards…" James sighed. "Well, they're Spaniards."

Hugh nodded, for he knew all too well what James meant. The Spaniards had not been trusted by a single British soldier since Talavera, where the British wounded had been left to their care, only for the Spanish to abandon them to the French.

"Worse even than the problems with our allies is Napoleon's spy network. They infiltrate us at every turn, it seems, knowing our moves almost before orders are issued. Wellington has ordered the most thorough investigation possible, but there is a leak somewhere high that cannot be stopped."

"Surely you don't mean a Staff Officer?" Hugh asked, deeply shocked at the thought that one so trusted could ever turn traitor.

"Of course not, Hugh—do try to keep up. I mean over here."

"You mean the War Office? Or the War Department? Or—" and though he could not credit it, there was only one option left "—or *Horse Guards*?"

"Indeed." James sank the contents of his glass and refilled it before sliding the decanter to Hugh, who sat still, stunned at the revelation. The number of officers assigned to Horse Guards was small—not counting the regiments, of course, whose offices were separate—which meant if there was a traitor in their ranks, it might be somebody he knew, or even somebody with whom he had worked these last four months.

"What can be done?" he asked.

James tossed off his glassful. "Wellington has set certain wheels in motion, though he will not say what. I only know that because I am on the Staff, and you must not mention it to a soul, Hugh."

"I am not entirely devoid of sense, James."

James grinned suddenly as he surveyed Hugh. "No, I suppose you are not. How is the beautiful Lady Emily?"

Hugh sighed as he placed his glass on the table. No matter how many times he heard it, James seemed unable to believe that Hugh's only interest in Emily was as a dearly loved sister, and that in return she viewed Hugh as a brother. "She is well."

"That's all you have to say? God, Hugh, you're such a looby! I have no idea how you of all people have managed it, but she most definitely has a partiality for you. You must make your move and press your suit before someone with more address sweeps her off her feet."

"Speaking of ladies, how is Miss Drury?" A carefully selected diversion usually worked with James.

It took another two glasses of port as well as some snuff before James could stop speaking of Miss Drury's charms long enough to allow them to join the ladies. Although Hugh could not quite believe that Elinor Drury, however admirable she may be, was the complete paragon that James's recitation would have her, he was pleased to learn of his brother's very real attachment. James had always had an eye for the ladies, and his pleasing disposition, easy company and good looks had assured him of a warm welcome wherever he went. To see him so bowled over that no one could compare to his affianced bride was a surprise indeed, but a welcome one. The fact their mother was similarly bowled over by Miss Drury's inheritance afforded Hugh some private amusement.

James's words about a possible traitor in the ranks stayed with Hugh as he walked back to Ryder Street later. He could scarcely credit it, thinking it much more likely that the leak was at the War Office. What man who had worn the King's uniform would betray it?

He became all the more convinced the spy was elsewhere as he considered the officers at Horse Guards. There was Colonel Badham, whose ill-humour was legendary. Surely if he were a spy, he would make himself a more conciliatory figure so he might fade into the background instead of being someone whose movements everyone tracked in order to avoid him? Then there were the colonels who worked so closely with the Adjutant General, the Quartermaster General and the Military Secretary. They all seemed men of honour to Hugh, although he supposed when he thought about it that he did not really know them. But it was inconceivable that such senior officers would ever do such a thing. There was Courtenay, but surely a spy would actually spend time in his place of work rather than saunter in for a short while every so often, complaining all the time as he did so. A spy would turn up early, work quietly and apparently conscientiously, and become so much part of the furniture that nobody would notice him. As Hugh thought about the officers at Horse Guards, he could not think of a single soul who fitted that description. The leak *must* be in the War Office.

Chapter Seven

Hugh presented himself at Half Moon Street the following evening for another night of gaiety. He would have cried off had James not been home, for he had spent quite enough time these last weeks dancing attendance upon his mother as she enjoyed the various delights of the Season, but it would be a chance to spend time with James. He might also find out if Emily's counsel had held sway at all with Sophia when it came to Stanton.

"Why are you out of uniform?" James demanded as Hugh was admitted to the drawing room. "You look positively drab."

"I know," Lady Fanshawe put in with a great sigh. "It is such a shame, but your brother never listens to a thing I say. Perhaps you can persuade him, James."

Hugh took his glass of sherry from Matthews with a smile of thanks. "I am in service dress all day, so I prefer not to spend my evenings in uniform too," he said by way of explanation. He knew James would never understand his true reason, for James revelled in being the centre of attention.

"That's a faradiddle and you know it," James returned indignantly. "Did you not do the same thing when campaigning?"

"But now I have a choice," Hugh said calmly, and turned to Sophia. "Another new gown, Sophia? It is most becoming."

Conversation successfully diverted, Hugh relaxed and enjoyed his sherry until it was time to leave for the ball that the Bonds were hosting to puff off their second daughter. His hopes that he would spend some time with James were quickly dashed, for his brother proved very much in demand for dancing as his regimentals had their inevitable effect. Hugh was left to circle the room, exchanging conversation with any number of people with whom he would have been happy never to have conversed. But as he was listening to the Dowager Countess of Royston yet again holding forth on her son's many qualities, he caught a flash of dark green through the throng, and his head rose as he searched. He had not been mistaken—Lindsay was across the other side of the room, looking as dashing as ever as he returned some young miss to her seat.

Hugh hastily extracted himself from the Dowager's clutches and attempted to carve a way through the crowds without looking too particular in his aim. He was foiled at every turn, for his attention was claimed with unusual enthusiasm as he went. An unguarded comment from Mrs Laversham betrayed the real reason for his sudden popularity—by falling into conversation with him, they hoped James might happen by and join them. He wondered at that, for it was known that James was to marry Miss Drury. Perhaps it was not matrimony they sought, but simply the diversion afforded by a good-looking young man in a scarlet coat.

Hugh was so turned about by the time the next set of dances ended that he had lost sight entirely of Lindsay. He retreated to the edge of the room, seeking a wall to stand against, only to find a hand placed in the small of his back and Lindsay's voice close against his ear. "Escaping already, Fanshawe? I cannot permit that. We must present a united front if we are to prevail."

Smiling, he turned his head. Lindsay looked even more handsome than Hugh had remembered, the silver buttons on his uniform coat sparkling in the light and his grey eyes filled with warmth along with the lazy amusement they so often showed.

"Does your united front permit a strategic regrouping?" Hugh asked.

"Music to my ears, Fanshawe. What have you in mind?"

"I was thinking a glass of punch and perhaps some cool air in the hall."

"With a tactical brain like that, I can't think how you have not yet been gazetted as general."

Procuring a glass of cold punch each, they escaped to the hall that ran the length of the house. It proved to be a busy thoroughfare, used by those seeking to move to the card room or the dressing room, or simply to take some cooler air.

In unspoken agreement, they moved to the far end and the large window onto Grosvenor Square, where they would not be disturbed. As Hugh turned to speak to Lindsay, he spied a familiar and extremely unwelcome figure reaching the top of the stairs. Stanton was here, and although Hugh thought he cut a most peculiar character in his striped waistcoat, he was fairly sure Sophia would be less discriminating in her taste.

"*Damn* it," he said, momentarily forgetting he was in company.

Lindsay followed his line of sight. "Ah," he said. "I had the impression the other night that Stanton was dangling after your sister."

"In a manner of speaking," Hugh concurred grimly.

"I suspected as much. Perhaps what gave me the first clue was when he likened her eyes to the beauty of stars sparkling like bright diamonds in a sky of black velvet and her smile to the sunrise that graced the dew of Eden's first dawn."

Hugh turned a revolted eye upon him. "No," he begged. "No, for God's sake, even *he* would not be so—so—"

"Lost in the poetical throes of passionate romance?" Lindsay suggested.

"I was about to say making a cake of himself," Hugh said. "But Sophia—I am sure that no matter how handsome she might think him, she would *never* hear such nonsense without succumbing to giggles."

"It's possible I exaggerated his words a little," Lindsay confessed. "Perhaps he merely mentioned how prettily her eyes shone and that her smile could light the room."

"Well, that's bad enough," Hugh said indignantly. "What sort of a fellow spouts such claptrap?"

"I take it you have never courted a lady," Lindsay said. "At least, not successfully."

Hugh choked on his punch. And then something, whether honesty or some inner demon, prompted him to answer. "No, I never have."

Lindsay fastened his eyes on Hugh's suddenly, and the look in them was such that Hugh found it difficult to breathe. Lindsay eventually looked away, leaving Hugh somewhat dazed.

When Lindsay spoke, it was as if the moment had never existed. "What are you going to do about Stanton?"

"I am not sure what I *can* do," Hugh confessed. "He has not gone beyond the line in any way, and although he knows I am watching, he sees me of no account due to my leg."

"Then he's a fool," Lindsay said strongly.

Hugh could not prevent the smile that tugged at his lips at Lindsay's words. But they were fated to enjoy no further private conversation for Hugh was being hailed from along the corridor. He looked up to find James making his way towards them.

"What are you doing skulking out here?" James started, and then caught sight of Lindsay standing slightly behind Hugh. "My apologies, sir—I did not see you there. Major James Fanshawe of the 7th Foot."

"Colonel Theo Lindsay, 95th Rifles. And to answer your question, Major, we are skulking out here to avoid the devious manoeuvres of those who would see their daughters married."

James laughed, the smile that adorned his face making him look even more like a figure from Greek myth than he already did. "In that case, I cry craven and will join you."

"You are already promised, so you are joining us under false pretences," Hugh pointed out. "Also, with your scarlet coat, you will be missed, and when your many admirers come searching for you, they will discover us."

"Are you saying the ladies find the scarlet more appealing than the green?" Lindsay asked. "I believe I have just been insulted."

"Yes, Hugh, please do explain to the colonel why I should be more in demand than he is."

"I think," Hugh said in a dignified manner, "I shall leave the two of you to settle the matter of regimental honour."

"You forget, brother, that you too have a horse in this race," James pointed out before turning back to Lindsay. "Are you on leave, sir?"

"Alas, no. I am waiting upon the Adjutant General's pleasure before I return to the regiment."

"You mean you're stuck at Horse Guards twiddling your thumbs?" James surmised.

"If you wish to put it that way, then I suppose I am."

"My condolences," James said.

"Oh, I don't know," Lindsay said, and as James took a drink from the glass in his hand, Lindsay ran his gaze over Hugh. "It has its compensations."

Hugh didn't know where to look, nor what to say. Thankfully James did not appear to notice anything amiss because he was continuing to talk, suddenly serious. "That fellow of yours who took out the French general at Corunna was an extraordinary shot."

"He is," Lindsay said. "As are they all."

James was all too pleased to agree with this—and Hugh knew that Lindsay was not being boastful in the least; the 95th were held in high regard—before plunging into further talk about recent happenings and people Hugh did not know but of whom James and Lindsay appeared to share some knowledge. He stood there, knowing he should excuse himself gracefully but unwilling to cede the field to James, despite the fact he and Lindsay were engaged in lively conversation.

Eventually he became aware that he was not only distinctly *de trop*, but also just a little pitiful still standing there, so he made his excuses in order to retreat. As he did so, Lindsay's hand fell upon his sleeve. "I have not forgotten, Fanshawe—we will arrange a time."

James looked between them, evidently surprised at the level of familiarity. It was some balm to Hugh's wounded feelings as he made his way back down the corridor, trying his best not to limp too badly just in case either of them were watching. It had been ever thus with James—his lively mind, generous spirit and good looks meant that all who encountered him fell a little under his spell. Hugh did not mind it usually, but he wished that, just this once, James would have kept his distance.

Chapter Eight

Hugh awoke the next morning to the quiet sounds of Murray in the dressing room. He lay in bed while Murray laid out all he would need to prepare for the day ahead of him and continued to laze as he was left in peace again. He felt in no hurry to report to Horse Guards and whatever stack of paperwork demanded his immediate attention today.

Instead he found himself thinking about Lindsay, about how he had enjoyed his company the previous evening, and how he had seen him again later, an elbow propped upon the mantel as he had engaged in deep conversation with James. Even when relaxed and unconscious of being observed, Lindsay was graceful. In that, he was so different from Hugh, who had not been known for his grace even before his injury. But the strange thing was that when Hugh was with him, he forgot about his leg.

He had often wished he could somehow have stayed with the regiment in the Peninsula, where injuries such as his were common and others were worse off, and nobody thought anything of those who were afflicted. It was the curiosity and distaste he encountered in London, and the way his mother had cried when she had first seen him walk, that had made him feel less than whole. Lindsay did not make him feel that way. In part, Hugh suspected it was because he too was a military man, yet Courtenay did not hesitate to flick barbed comments at him on occasion, and James, while meaning so well, made Hugh all the more self-conscious because of the very real difference between them. James had tucked his arm through Hugh's last night and attempted to walk with him, doubtless thinking he was helping Hugh but actually pulling him off balance and making his progress even more awkward. Thankfully Sophia had demanded James's attention almost immediately, meaning he had left Hugh to his own devices once more.

Hugh frowned slightly as he rubbed his leg, which was aching from another long evening spent standing. He had not realised Sophia was beginning to make a public spectacle of herself in refusing to rebuff Stanton's improper advances. For Lindsay to be aware of what had passed between them meant that others too might have overheard. He remembered Lindsay and Emily had stood up together beside Stanton and Sophia at the Trents' ball, which presumably was where this conversation had occurred. And then he drew in a breath as he realised—perhaps that was why Lindsay had stepped in, inviting her to dance and escorting her to supper, all to prevent Stanton's attentions becoming even more particular, and Sophia, well-behaved as she was, had no alternative but to accept Lindsay's company with good grace and apparent enjoyment.

He was not sure why Lindsay would put himself to so much trouble, yet now he had thought of it, he was reasonably certain that was what he had done. Hugh could not decide why he felt able to accept Lindsay's intervention and feel grateful for it, rather than humiliated that he had been unable to step in himself. He thought perhaps it was because Lindsay made everything seem easy and natural between them. In that, as in all else, he was exceptional.

Exceptional as he was, there were still many things about Theo Lindsay that left Hugh confused. He had thought last night, when Lindsay's eyes had travelled with intent over his body while he spoke of compensations, that he was indeed interested in Hugh in the way that Hugh was in him. His presence at the molly house made it clear that he had an interest in men in general. What remained unclear was whether he had any interest in *Hugh*. Why should he, after all? Yet Hugh could not shake the feeling—perhaps no more than a hope—that there was something between them. As he thought again of the way Lindsay had looked at him, the intent in his eyes, the way his uniform hugged his powerful body, he found he was becoming aroused.

He threw back the blankets and got out of bed. It was one thing to wish and hope, but another thing entirely to allow those thoughts free rein in a way that meant he would never again be able to look Colonel Lindsay in the face. He turned his attention to dressing for the day, and his plight slowly eased.

Upon arrival at Horse Guards, he found a letter addressed to him upon his desk. He discovered on opening it that it was from Colonel Lindsay; he had been called out of town for a few days but would greatly enjoy the company of Captain Fanshawe for dinner in his lodgings upon his return on Friday of that week. Hugh could not help but smile as he folded the letter and placed it in his pocket. Lindsay had been as good as his word and remembered the casual commitment he had made to Hugh.

As he sharpened his quill in preparation for the day's work ahead of him, Hugh suddenly realised it did not say much for their security that Lindsay—or somebody acting on his behalf—had been able to leave the letter on Hugh's desk while their office was unoccupied. Before the conversation with James, he had always thought the sentries on duty were enough to control access to the building.

Realising the ease with which Lindsay had come and gone during his time there, he began to wonder. While it was entirely proper for Lindsay to have access, Hugh did not know how many less-trustworthy types might enjoy the same ease of movement through the building. Regarding the ordered paperwork on his desk, and the messy piles that covered almost the entire surface of Courtenay's, he wondered if they should put a lock upon their door.

He mentioned his thoughts to Courtenay when he finally appeared.

"A lock? What has prompted such an excess of caution?"

Mindful of James's warning to mention their conversation to no one, Hugh shrugged. "It was an idle thought, no more."

Courtenay's eyes were sharp upon his face. "Something must have prompted it. Even *your* prudence is not usually quite so pronounced."

Damn it, Hugh really should have thought this through before raising it. "I arrived to find a letter on my desk," he said, for Courtenay would see through any dissembling. "It made me wonder who has access to our office."

"You fear you will be robbed blind here at Horse Guards?" Courtenay helped himself to a pinch of snuff as his eyebrows raised mockingly, before offering his box to Hugh.

"It was an idle thought," Hugh disclaimed, declining the snuff with a shake of his head.

"If you would feel safer, then by all means, go ahead, my dear Fanshawe," Courtenay said. "I would hate for you to sit there quaking in your boots lest some footpad happen by and make off with one of your valuable requests for leave."

Hugh said nothing further. It had been foolish of him to raise the subject in the first place. He supposed any spy worth his salt would be able to circumvent a locked door with ease. In addition, if a spy felt his presence was suspected, he would act with more caution and be more difficult to catch.

Once he realised that, he was thankful he had mentioned his blockheaded idea only to Courtenay.

Hugh settled to his work. If he smiled occasionally as the paper in his pocket rustled, well, it made the day pass more swiftly.

On Friday afternoon, Hugh left Horse Guards earlier than was his habit and took himself to Half Moon Street. He hoped to see James, because he would welcome his thoughts on the ease of access to their offices. As James was not familiar with Horse Guards—his precise expressed wish had been to have his entrails dug out by a French Eagle rather than darken the doorstep of the place—he would presume that all there was safe. It was not necessarily the case that somebody there was a spy—it might be that somebody not on the staff was gaining access.

Hugh's disappointment at learning from Matthews that Major Fanshawe had gone out was somewhat ameliorated on being informed that *Miss* Fanshawe was home. His conversation with Lindsay about Stanton had been troubling him and he had determined that he must speak to Sophia, no matter Emily's strictures on the matter. While he was sure he could trust Lindsay's discretion completely, and had his own reasons to know that was the case, for somebody outside the family to be aware of her encouragement of Stanton's attentions meant things had gone too far. He was mindful of what Emily had said and determined to be subtle rather than let loose the broadside he wished about that gentleman's morals and behaviour.

First, however, there was the delicate matter of finding a way to raise the subject.

"Did you enjoy yourself last night?" he asked.

"Oh yes, it was such a crush, and best of all, no Marquess present for Mama to fix her eye upon."

"I'm sure you didn't lack for other partners."

"Everyone there was most gallant in soliciting a dance," Sophia said. "I could have wished some of them had paid more attention to Lavinia, but then, she has given away her heart so she would doubtless have declined any offers."

"Miss Williams has a suitor?" Hugh tried to cover his surprise, although he suspected he was not entirely successful.

"There is one gentleman who appears to have a very particular interest in her, but it is to no avail—she is quite set upon a military gentleman."

"They do not always make the best of husbands, you know, with so much time overseas."

"So I have told her, but there is one particular military gentleman who has stolen her heart."

Hugh's eyebrows raised interrogatively, and then the true meaning of Sophia's speaking look was borne in upon him. "No," he said, horrified. "No, dash it, Sophia—you can't mean..."

"But, Hugh, how could you think otherwise after the gallantry of your heroic rescue at the Fitzroys' ball? You won her heart there and then, and everything you have done since has determined her that you are the best, the kindest, the *noblest* of gentlemen, with a visage to cast Adonis himself into the shade." Sophia's voice was shaking as she reached the end of her paean to Hugh's attributes.

"Sophia!" Hugh was horrified. "You cannot encourage this nonsense."

"Oh, but what could be better than my best friend and my best brother becoming husband and wife?" Sophia said, but there was enough of a mischievous sparkle in her eyes for Hugh to realise she was not fully serious. "Do not be alarmed, dear brother—I suspected those would be your feelings and I will convey to her the true state of your affections."

"*Sophia.*" Hugh could not understand how his sister had become so lost to all notion of proper behaviour. "You can't do such a thing. She will be mortified you have told me."

"You misunderstand me, Hugh. I will explain to her your tragic circumstances—doomed to be violently in love with Lady Emily, lost to all reason and driven to the point of madness by your passion for her, taking on any and all challengers for her hand in duels to the death. But alas, it is all in vain because Lady Emily remains faithful to the memory of her late, dear husband, for whom she mourns every day and cannot wait to join in the grave. It is quite possible Lavinia might enter into a consumptive state and die from a broken heart because you do not return her affections, but I am sure an unforeseen hero will appear and save her from such a lonely fate."

Hugh regarded her with a mixture of horror and fascination. "Have you been borrowing novels from the circulating library again?" he asked suspiciously.

She gave him a sunny smile. "Not I, this time, but Mrs Radcliffe's stories are Lavinia's very favourite."

He shook his head in wonder. "You really are a brat."

"Well, that is not at all gentlemanly of you, Hugh. I am most disappointed."

Her pout was almost enough to make him laugh, but then he recalled himself and what it was he had hoped to talk to her about. "Sophia, there is something I must mention to you."

The laughter in her face faded at his tone. "Yes?"

"Your standing up so often with Stanton is beginning to cause talk," he said. "I think it advisable for you not to do so every time you see him." There, even Emily would have to allow that was a diplomatic approach, suggesting rather than forbidding.

"Do you indeed?" Sophia's chin was up and her eyes sparkled dangerously. "Well, I think it is up to me with whom I dance, and all the old tabbies who have nothing better to do than to gossip about it can go and jump in the Thames!"

Hugh stared at her for an appalled moment, and then he spoke his mind, all thoughts of forbearance fled. "He is a ramshackle fellow with a reputation for dalliance, and you do yourself and your reputation no good by welcoming his advances. Let me speak plainly, Sophia—you are very beautiful, but you have no fortune that would tempt a man of his character to marriage."

"And *you* are such a model of duty and honour and propriety and—and *orderliness* before all else!" she hurled at him. "You cannot understand a man like Ralph, how passionate and *sensitive* he is! It is not his fault that the rest of the *ton* do not see him for the man he is, judging him instead on outmoded notions of what they think is *proper*."

"You call him by his *name*? Sophia, can you not see how wrong this is? He is taking advantage of your feelings to lure you into behaviour that does not become you. And you may think me stuffy, but do you really wish to be connected to a man who, in your own words, has no notion of duty or honour or propriety?"

Tears sprang to Sophia's eyes and spilled down her cheeks. "I *knew* you wouldn't understand," she accused him, her voice wobbling perilously. "You have never been in love, and you cannot understand what it means."

Hugh took a step towards her, but she pushed past him. "Leave me *alone*!"

The door slammed behind her. Hugh stood on his own in the drawing room and wondered what had just happened.

Chapter Nine

Later that evening, Hugh presented himself at Lindsay's set of chambers at Albany, little more than five minutes' walk from his own lodgings. He was in morning dress as the invitation had made it clear this was to be an informal occasion and was momentarily relieved on seeing his host that his presumption had been correct.

And then the full effect of Lindsay's attire burst in upon him. He was wearing an exquisitely fitted blue coat, beneath which was a cream waistcoat embroidered in gold, tightly fitting buff pantaloons and gleaming tasselled Hessians. Hugh's greeting died on his lips as he drank in the picture before him. Thankfully Lindsay said nothing about his sudden lapse in manners, although there was amusement in his eyes.

Hugh finally recovered himself enough to take a seat on the sofa as invited, and Lindsay's man served them both with sherry before dinner. Lindsay's set of chambers was luxurious—larger than Hugh's and ideally appointed.

"As you are only here temporarily, I had thought you would put up at a hotel rather than take a set," Hugh said, indicating the gracefully proportioned room.

Lindsay stretched out beside him, warming his boots at the fire. "I keep this set permanently for whenever I am in London." He took a delicate sip of his sherry. "I find it affords greater privacy than a hotel."

Hugh shot a questioning glance at Lindsay, and found Lindsay was looking at him in a most particular way. Surely even *he* could not be misreading this. He swallowed. "I imagine it must."

"Were you able to conclude your business satisfactorily?" he asked, when the silence between them had gone on a little too long to be entirely comfortable.

Lindsay glanced away. "I did," he said. "I was entrusted with a message to Colonel Murray of the Monmouth Light. They're marching reinforcements out to meet Wellington, but we have wind that the French know of this and will set up an ambush, so we're sending them to Coimbra by ship instead. It was felt inadvisable to entrust such sensitive information to a letter and as I had, apparently, nothing better to do with my time, I was dispatched to Colchester." He affected a shudder. "Ghastly place—entirely uncivilised with no comfort to be found anywhere. No wonder the plague tried to wipe it from the face of the Earth."

"I can see how it must have compared unfavourably to a draughty bivouac on the Castilian plain," Hugh agreed.

"You have no idea. Do you know, the wine they served in the Mess was *mislabelled*?"

"Dear God, no!"

"Yes. And what is even worse, my host did not appear to notice."

Hugh adopted a suitably grave expression. "It was evidently vital you shook the dust from your feet just as soon as you could."

Lindsay levelled a narrowed glance at Hugh. "I think you are not taking my travails seriously enough, Fanshawe," he complained. "I have been quite overset by venturing into the wilds."

The meal that was served to them appeared to put Lindsay on the mend, however. It was a splendid repast, accompanied by a particularly good—and most definitely not mislabelled—

Moscatel. As a result, when the port was finished and they had repaired to the sitting room, Hugh was feeling comfortably satisfied, warm and full of good cheer.

He sat upon the sofa. Lindsay, having dismissed his man, brought him a glass of brandy and sat beside him.

"Did I miss any scandal in my absence, Hugh?"

Hugh froze at the unexpected sound of his first name on Lindsay's lips. When he met Lindsay's gaze, it was steady and friendly, and there was something else in it also. He placed his glass upon the side table, because otherwise Lindsay—*Theo*—might see the sudden slight tremor in his hand.

"I believe the *ton* survived tolerably well without you," he said, "although I am sure your absence has resulted in several maidens' decline, Theo."

There was a very good reason why Hugh had joined the army, and it had nothing to do with wishing to fight Napoleon. He entirely lacked the easy social graces of his brothers and sister. Unlike Theo's natural tone, his use of Theo's first name was ugly and clumsy, and seemed almost to vibrate in the air for minutes afterwards to ensure it had drawn enough attention to itself. He could not hold Theo's gaze.

"I'm sure you stepped into the breach heroically," Theo said. He placed his hand upon Hugh's thigh. The shock of being touched and the warmth that began to come through the wool of his pantaloons left Hugh breathing unevenly. "There is something I wished to discuss with you, Hugh. I have not forgotten my promise to introduce you to other gentlemen, should you so wish."

"I—thank you, no," Hugh managed. His mind was a fog, one in which he could not find his way. All he could think of was the weight and warmth of Theo's touch, and the quiver of excitement deep in his stomach. He wet his lips and tried again. "I have no interest—that is to say—"

"Good," Theo murmured. "I would not wish for you to kiss me only because you lacked alternatives."

As Hugh struggled for breath, Theo leaned in, his hand moving to cup Hugh's jaw and his thumb brushing his cheek. And then his lips met Hugh's. They were gentle and warm, and possibly the most wonderful thing Hugh had ever known. Theo pulled back after a moment to look at him, his thumb stroking over Hugh's lower lip, lightly, yet firmly enough to have Hugh's mouth opening slightly under his touch. He moistened his lip with his tongue where Theo had touched it.

Theo's eyes changed, growing intent, and he leaned the last few inches to kiss Hugh again. This time his mouth moved against Hugh's, coaxing, and when Hugh followed Theo's guidance, he found his lips were parted enough for Theo's tongue to slide into his mouth. Arousal shocked through Hugh, and the surprised noise he made had Theo pulling back again. Laughter was in his eyes, but it did not seem that he was laughing *at* Hugh, precisely.

"I take it that was to your liking," he said.

"God, yes," Hugh said breathlessly and leaned forward, wanting more. This time when Theo kissed him, Hugh slid his hand into Theo's hair and held him close as Theo's tongue pushed into his mouth, slick and strong, setting wild feelings racing through Hugh. He finally gathered the courage to return the kiss, moving his tongue uncertainly against Theo's, causing Theo to make an approving sound in his throat.

Hugh had had carnal relations several times before, but never had he kissed anyone, nor been kissed—whores did not do that, and he had never set himself up with a ladybird. He wondered now why he had been so foolish, because he could have had this for all of these years. When Theo finally drew back, pressing a last few brief kisses against Hugh's mouth, he thought perhaps it was not so much the kissing that was wonderful as the fact it was Theo.

Although Theo had drawn away, his hand still cupped Hugh's jaw and his thumb kept passing over Hugh's lower lip as though he could not let go completely. He studied Hugh's face. Hugh stared at him. He had no clue what Theo was thinking, but he hoped so very much that this was not an end of it. He wanted Theo close again like that. He wanted Theo even closer, to touch him and be touched by him.

Theo nodded slightly to himself, as though he had made up his mind. "Will you come to bed?"

"Yes." Hugh said it instantly, and he knew there was no other answer it was possible for him to give.

Theo stood and held out his hand to Hugh. He did not pull him up as other well-meaning gentlemen had tried before—he merely provided his hand and arm for Hugh to use as leverage, adjusting as necessary as Hugh gained his feet. Once Hugh was standing, Theo led the way down the corridor and through the doorway into his bedchamber, where the candles were already lit and the fire had evidently been alight long enough to warm the room nicely.

Hugh suddenly realised, and stopped just inside the room. "Your man?"

Theo smiled and stepped in close to Hugh. "My man sees little and hears less," he said, reaching out to push the door closed behind them. "There is nothing to worry about, I assure you, unless it is how I can untie your confounded neckcloth. God's sake, Hugh—what were you thinking with such a complicated construction?" But his hands gave lie to his words, easily undoing the Osbaldeston which Hugh had so painstakingly tied earlier that evening and lifting the length of material from around his neck to toss it carelessly in the direction of a chair. "I daresay your valet is an excellent man who will be appalled to the depths of his being by the insult I am about to inflict on your clothing," he continued, as he removed Hugh's coat with an ease that belied its close fit, and then began to undo the buttons of his waistcoat.

"I am sure he will somehow survive the horror," Hugh said, but his attempt to match Theo's casual tone was undone by his breathlessness. Theo was stripping him bare, the way his eyes so often did. Except this was—oh, God, this was so very different from that, because Hugh's waistcoat was open and Theo was touching him through his soft lawn shirt, and Hugh could not bear it any longer. Seizing hold of Theo's coat, Hugh pulled him in close and kissed him.

Kissing Theo was even better than it had been upon the sofa because Theo was pressed against him, and it became quite clear to Hugh that Theo was in a similar state of excitement to his own. As he felt that, Hugh made a sound into Theo's mouth that he instantly wished he could deny. But instead of amusing Theo, it spurred him on to kiss Hugh more deeply, more urgently, and to rid him of his waistcoat entirely. He finally pulled back and unbuttoned Hugh's shirt, before pulling it off. Then he looked at Hugh, at the body that had been revealed to him, with eyes that were dark and wanting.

"You're wearing too many clothes," Hugh said, and found that his voice was hoarse.

Theo instantly began to rectify that fact, treating his clothes with as little care as he had Hugh's. Hugh wanted to help but suspected if he did so, he would only slow Theo down. He also wanted to watch Theo's nimble, confident fingers at work on his fastenings and to see what lay beneath his clothes. When Theo lifted his shirt over his head and dropped it onto the floor—any pretence he was aiming for a chair had long since gone—it was all Hugh could do not to gasp.

Because Theo...Theo was *perfect*. He was like the marble statues in the temple to Priapus at Somerset House, those beautiful young men who were composed of smooth planes of muscle which Hugh had thought reflected the longings of their sculptors more than reality. Theo was proof that men really *could* be so beautiful.

Hugh couldn't help himself—he stepped forward and pressed his fingers to the smooth, warm skin of Theo's chest, feeling the way Theo's heart raced under his cautious exploration. He looked at Theo and found he was intently watching Hugh's hand upon him, but then he looked up at Hugh. He leaned in and took Hugh's mouth in a kiss that left him dizzy and unsure if he would ever be able to breathe again.

That question was answered when Theo finally raised his head and pressed his hand lightly against the fall of Hugh's pantaloons. Hugh gasped and pushed into the touch.

"Your boots need to come off," Theo said. "Sit down."

Hugh sat down upon the bed, and Theo knelt before him to remove his Hessians, particularly careful with his left one, before standing up once more and encouraging Hugh further back upon the bed. When Hugh's hands went to the buttons of his pantaloons, Theo pushed them away and undid them himself.

Under Theo's guidance, Hugh raised his hips to allow Theo to draw down his pantaloons and his drawers, and guide them all the way off his legs, along with his stockings. For an instant, Hugh wanted to close his eyes, because being naked like this in front of Theo meant he could hide nothing. But then he saw the way Theo looked at him, his breath coming more quickly as he did so, and the racing of Hugh's heart was no longer from self-consciousness.

It took tremendous self-restraint, but Hugh managed to keep himself from touching him as Theo sat upon the edge of the bed, the muscles in his back shifting as he pulled off his own Hessians. He then stood and unfastened his pantaloons, and stripped off the rest of his clothing with a graceful economy of movement. Hugh's mouth dried as he stared at Theo, for he was completely naked, very obviously aroused, and the heat in his gaze was a world away from the cold, lifeless marble statues to which Hugh had just been likening him.

Theo settled on the bed above him, his arms and legs taking most of his weight, and brought them together at the hips and the mouth. Feeling Theo against him like that, all restraint left Hugh. He pulled Theo down on top of him, until they were pressed together, kissing and moving against each other, and Hugh was able finally to touch Theo wherever he wished. It turned out he wished to touch Theo *everywhere.* Theo was as strong as Hugh had thought, his body hard with muscle. His tongue pushed deeply into Hugh's mouth, echoing the moves he was making with his hips, pushing their yards together.

It was better than Hugh's wildest imaginings, but there was still one thing he wanted even more than this. He wanted to *touch* Theo. He reached down between them, Theo lifting his hips slightly so Hugh could wrap his hand round Theo's firm, hot flesh. The jolt Theo gave, the way he stopped kissing Hugh and instead simply breathed against his neck, making little sounds into Hugh's skin, let Hugh know he was doing this right. It was like nothing Hugh had ever known before, better even than finding his own pleasure. Well, almost—he found he had to rethink that when Theo recovered himself enough to take Hugh in hand in turn, which had Hugh pushing up wildly, desperate for the curve of his hand and the perfect friction of the slight calluses on Theo's fingers.

It seemed no time at all before it was over, their releases commingled on their skins. Hugh had clutched at Theo as it came upon him, needing an anchor as he fought not to cry out at how it felt to be with Theo like this.

They lay there a little while before Theo untangled himself from Hugh and settled beside him with a slight, breathless laugh. "Had I any idea what enthusiasm lay beneath that extremely proper exterior of yours, I should not have waited so long."

Hugh flushed slightly, and Theo instantly leaned up upon his elbow, his fingers closing on Hugh's jaw and guiding him to look at Theo. "That was not a criticism," he said. "It appears I have a previously unsuspected weakness for propriety." He lay back down again with a satisfied-sounding sigh, looking at the ceiling above them. "You'll stay, I take it?"

"Your servants—"

"Will doubtless think my charms have sadly diminished if you refuse."

Hugh frowned as he looked at Theo, not understanding him.

"One of my reasons for sometimes frequenting molly houses is that I can make it known if I am seeking to take on any new servants," Theo said. "I do not question what activities they might enjoy in their free time, and they do not question mine. I believe it to be a rather good arrangement."

There was no gainsaying that. But...

"Do you frequent molly houses often?" Hugh asked, because Theo had said there were risks in doing so. If he felt a slight sting at the thought of it, that was undoubtedly due to his worry for Theo's safety.

Theo rolled over so that he was facing Hugh and made himself comfortable upon his pillow. "Not so very often, but sometimes. I prefer men who use their bodies to work or to fight, not the dandies and the tulips of the *ton*. But do not be tempted into doing the same thing, Hugh. It is safe for me—I have powerful friends. I could not say the same for you if there were to be a raid."

The slight sting that Hugh had felt increased tenfold at the realisation that, despite what they had just done together, Theo expected Hugh to go looking for other company. Which must mean Theo would do so. He had no idea why he should have thought otherwise, unless he had somehow stupidly thought that Theo's invitation for him to stay meant more than merely not wishing to be disturbed by Hugh getting up and dressing himself. Hugh looked away from Theo and found himself examining the embroidery on the silk counterpane beneath them.

"There is another good reason you should not go to such a place, of course, and that is because if you were to fix your fancy upon anyone else, I should be obliged to call him out," Theo said. "Indeed, from the attention your brief sojourn amongst us attracted that night, I believe I might spend some considerable time involved in duels. You were quite the hit."

Hugh was unhappily aware he was being made fun of, yet he could not let such an accusation pass without trying to defend himself. "I'm not a *flirt.*"

Theo choked on a laugh. "No, I can see that," he agreed. "You are, however..." And then he paused, surveying Hugh, who stared back at him, confused. "You are very *Hugh*," he declared at last, and pulled Hugh against him. "And have rendered me entirely inarticulate, it seems."

Hugh didn't understand what Theo meant, but he relaxed in the warmth of his hold, deciding to pay no heed to his funning. He could not stop from touching Theo now he was finally allowed to, setting his hands drifting over Theo's body and following the lines of hard muscles beneath the skin.

He traced the long, ugly scar that ran down Theo's left arm. "Sword?" he asked, because he had seen too many examples of that type of wound not to recognise it.

"Ciudad Rodrigo."

That had been a bad business. Every battle was a bad business, for that matter. It was something on which Hugh did not care to dwell. Perhaps Theo felt the same, for they both fell silent.

Hugh must have fallen asleep, because he came to with a start to find Theo had moved. He was kneeling further down the bed, his hand resting on Hugh's bad leg.

He glanced up as Hugh startled awake. "I need to know what it is we are dealing with," he said, by way of explanation. "Tell me, how far are you able to bend your knee?"

Theo was entirely matter-of-fact about his investigations, his hands upon Hugh's leg moving it to discover its limits, bending it, straightening it, checking all the time how what he was doing felt to Hugh. By the time Theo was through with him, having explored the entire range of movement he still had and traced the scars from where the surgeon had cut open his leg even further to remove every last piece of broken bone, Hugh felt no embarrassment at Theo knowing the extent of his unsoundness, nor feeling how weak the lower leg was.

"Excellent," Theo concluded enthusiastically, having conducted an examination more painstaking than Hugh had received from any man of medicine. "Although I believe, to be entirely sure of my findings, I should engage in a thorough testing." The glinting grin he gave had Hugh's heart beating harder, and an instant later Theo surged up the bed, taking Hugh's mouth in a kiss while his hands explored with purpose.

Their coming together was just as urgent as the first time, and Hugh was soon lost, with Theo's body moving against him in such a way. And then he held him close while Theo gasped out his completion.

Hugh was sure he could not want for greater happiness than this.

Chapter Ten

Hugh came slowly to awareness, not understanding why his face appeared to be pressed against something solid and warm. He jerked fully awake as he realised—he was in bed with Theo, his cheek resting against Theo's chest, and strong arms around him. Hearing a metallic scraping sound, he realised that was what had woken him. He turned and saw in the dim morning light that Theo's man was engaged in cleaning the grate.

Theo's arms tightened, and Hugh drew his eyes away from the fireplace and looked up into his face. Theo looked as if he had been awake for some time, alert and fully aware of all that was happening around him.

"Sleep," Theo said quietly. "All is well."

Theo's body was sleep-warm against Hugh's, the hold of his arms somehow reassuring, and Hugh gradually relaxed from his rude awakening. His eyes closed, and he didn't hear the servant leave the room.

When he awoke some time later, daylight was streaming through the window, from which the curtains had been drawn back. A fire was burning brightly in the hearth, and Theo was sitting up on his side of the bed, his hands behind his head. He was watching with some amusement Hugh's sleepy blinking into full wakefulness. As Hugh stirred, his leg made known its usual morning ache, and he rubbed it beneath the covers as he wished Theo a good morning, his voice still somewhat thick with sleep.

He wondered if he should feel self-conscious about the fact he was naked and in bed with an equally naked Theo, but he would not change things for the world. The covers were pooled around Theo's waist, revealing the muscled perfection of his body and causing Hugh to wonder precisely what the etiquette for this particular situation was. It was not one in which he had previously found himself, and he did not know if tackling Theo, who happened to be both his host and a senior officer, to the bed and touching him the way he wished to was quite the done thing. Perhaps he should wait for Theo to make the first move. Or perhaps, he realised with dawning dismay, what had happened last night was not to be repeated.

"Good God, Hugh—the working of your brain is louder even than your snores. And at this hour? Have you no consideration?"

Hugh relaxed then, remembering this was *Theo*. His host, yes, a senior officer, yes, but *Theo*.

Before he could take advantage of that realisation and follow his wishes to reacquaint himself with Theo in the most intimate way, Theo frowned slightly. "Your leg?"

Hugh realised he was still rubbing it, and stopped. "It's nothing of consequence," he said. "It merely tends to make its presence known after a night of inaction."

Theo's eyebrows climbed as Hugh spoke. "You realise I could take that as some sort of a challenge," he said, but even as he teased, he threw back the covers so he could see better. "Allow me."

He moved so that he was able to take the offending limb between his large, warm hands, and slowly begin to rub. As he did so, Hugh sighed and lay back upon the pillow. He didn't know what magic Theo had in his hands, but what he was doing was a hundredfold better than his own attempts to ease the cursed thing. As the ache that so often nagged at him disappeared entirely, he became aware that Theo's touch was no longer designed simply to ease his discomfort.

It was not much longer before Hugh was gasping under Theo's attentions, his hands clutching at Theo as he spent himself.

Some hours later, Hugh was established comfortably in Theo's sitting room, reading *The Times.* They had arisen rather late and enjoyed a relaxed breakfast before perusing the day's newspapers, which had been laid out awaiting them. Apparently Theo took a copy of each of the newspapers instead of reading just one, as Hugh was wont to do. Hugh was clad in what he knew Murray would bewail as the *ruins* of his shirt, pantaloons and stockings from the previous night, as well as one of Theo's dressing gowns, a magnificent creation of frogged gold-and-crimson brocaded silk. Theo, resplendent in a gown of quilted blue satin, was deep in another newspaper.

"For God's sake!"

Hugh looked up from *The Times* to see Theo tossing his copy of *The Daily Chronicle* aside. He sounded, and looked, extremely irritated.

"What's wrong?"

"Damned newspapers and damned leaks. Would you believe somebody has supplied to that wretched publication a copy of one of Wellington's circulars? I grant he is an ill-tempered martinet at times, but they twist things to make him sound a prating fool into the bargain."

Perhaps it was as well Theo was not in London often, for it was depressingly common to read that sort of thing in the newspaper. People didn't hesitate to use military matters for political gain, regardless of whether or not they had any comprehension of those matters.

"There's no way of tracing the leak?" Hugh asked, though he thought he already knew the answer.

"None. The document was only for the commanding officers, but of course copies will have reached the regimental files. You know as well as I the number of people who havc access to those."

Hugh did indeed.

"Next we see, they will be publishing the revised route of the Monmouth Light reinforcements," Theo grumbled.

"No. Even the newspapers would not risk military defeat for political gain."

Theo snorted. "Some days I can't decide whether such innocence in you is charming or dangerous," he said, sounding ill-tempered still. He stood up suddenly, picked up the newspaper and cast it onto the fire. "That's the best place for it. Now, what shall we do today, Captain Fanshawe? Taylor tells me it is temperate enough to make a ride in the Park a pleasure rather than a madcap excursion."

"I no longer ride," Hugh confessed awkwardly.

Theo stared at him. "Why? Your knee bends, after a fashion, and your thigh grips—extremely well, if my memory is to be trusted—and I know for a fact there is absolutely nothing wrong with your seat."

Hugh blushed at the images conjured by Theo's words even as he tried to wrest his mind back to the matter in hand. "I daresay I could manage, but I can't see how to mount."

"We shall have to resolve that situation," Theo declared. "You can't be in London in the Season and not make your appearance in the Park. More importantly, you can't desert me to make my appearance there alone and be besieged by matchmaking harpies. Come along, Hugh—your heroism is required."

And before Hugh knew entirely what he was doing, he found himself fully dressed in last night's clothes and sent on his way to his lodgings in Ryder Street so he might shave and change into clothes suitable for riding before meeting Theo at the mews. Hugh had been uneasy at that suggestion, knowing the trouble to which he was putting Theo when usually he would have his horse brought to him, but Theo would have none of it.

"It's about time I checked in on Joseph and ensured he hasn't seduced any stable lads," he said. "Or rather, as I know the likelihood of that, that he has not seduced too many all at once."

When Hugh reached the mews, he found Theo deep in conversation with a man who looked to be middle-aged. He was bow-legged, and what little remained of his hair was dark brown in colour. This was Joseph, Theo's groom, and Hugh thought that Theo must have been roasting him about his carnal appetite, for he seemed a very taciturn fellow.

Joseph brought Leander out for Hugh when bidden. He was a neat-looking bay of about sixteen hands with a white star on his forehead and appeared most taken with Joseph's pockets, as though looking for a treat.

"Away with you now," Joseph scolded him.

As if he understood, the beast heaved a sigh and stood quietly while Hugh approached him, unsure just what Theo had in mind for getting him up there. It was soon clear, for he was bidden to bend his left knee, so far as he was able, and Theo cupped his hands beneath it. On a count of three, with the propulsion of his sound leg and a strong boost from Theo, Hugh found himself in the saddle with a minimum of fuss. The awkwardness he felt at being treated like a lady faded as he realised only Theo, Joseph and Leander had witnessed the entire event, and none of them had paid it any heed.

Seeing that Hugh had gathered his reins and was adjusting his stirrups, Joseph disappeared into the stables. He returned leading a large chestnut with a bold blaze down its face. Once Theo had swung himself lightly up into the chestnut's saddle, Joseph moved the few steps over to Hugh and offered him a whip.

"Might be handy, sir," he said, and it did not escape Hugh that he was offering the whip to his left hand. He had no idea if he would be able to use his left leg to guide the horse; the whip would be something with which he could exert any pressure needed. He took it with gratitude, but when he thanked Joseph, the man merely shuffled back silently in the direction of the stables. Like master, like groom—they shared a matter-of-fact approach that made nothing of Hugh's problem while finding a way around it.

As they negotiated the busy streets on the way to Hyde Park, Hugh found it difficult—nay, impossible—to stop smiling. He had missed riding, but more than that, it was a wonderful feeling to cover ground easily and at a good pace, without pain or effort.

They had not been in the Park long when Hugh spied a familiar-looking figure in a barouche which was pulled up at the edge of the Row. The great congregation of gentlemen gathered around it confirmed who the occupant must be. Emily saw their approach, and he noted the surprise in her face, followed by a smile of such brilliance that most of her admirers were unable to prevent themselves from turning to see what had prompted it.

Emily said something then, which he was sure was all graciousness yet left them in no doubt they'd been dismissed. By the time he and Theo reached her and made their greetings, the gentlemen in question had unwillingly melted away. Hugh could understand their reluctance to leave, for Emily looked as lovely as ever in a gown of green silk, with a small straw hat placed at a fetchingly rakish angle on her ringlets.

"Hugh, what a truly delightful surprise it is to see you here," she declared, the smile on her face matched by the happiness in her eyes. "And so excellently mounted, too."

He stroked Leander's strong neck. "He is Colonel Lindsay's horse."

"I see," Emily said, although he had no idea what it was she saw. Her eyes were lit with amusement, as though at a private joke. "It is most generous of you, Colonel Lindsay."

"Pure self-interest," he replied promptly. "I require protection from predatory mothers. I fully expect Captain Fanshawe to immolate himself upon the matrimonial altar in my defence should it be required."

"Is *that* what you expect of him?" Emily murmured, and their eyes met before she turned her attention back to Hugh. "Now, Hugh—we must have words. You have done exactly what I advised against and spoken to Sophia, haven't you?"

Thoughts of anything that was not Theo had slipped from Hugh's mind over the past day, and it took him a little while to remember what Emily was speaking about. And then he recollected the disastrous conversation with Sophia. "You've spoken to her?"

"I met her walking with Miss Williams earlier and took them up for a turn around the Park, during which she confided to me that, although you are an excellent brother in general, when it comes to this you are an insensitive block who will *never* understand the emotions of one truly in love."

Hugh sighed and his shoulders slumped. "Why is she so intransigent?"

"I might ask the same of you," Emily returned with spirit. "I was making such progress too. I had her agreeing with me just the other day that although disordered hair might look to be romantic and handsome, the very fact it was unbrushed meant one could not be sure *what* might be living in it."

Theo laughed. "Lady Emily, I feel almost sorry for the man upon whom your disapproval falls. I can only pray it never does so upon me."

"Then do not give me a reason," she responded, eyes sharp upon his face.

Laughter faded from Theo's face as he returned Emily's gaze, until finally he looked away across the Park.

"So Miss Williams also knows of her attachment?" Hugh said, dismayed as the full extent of the situation was borne in upon him.

"They are bosom friends, after all," Emily said, her eyes returning to Hugh. "Don't tell me that you and Robert didn't share everything, for I know that to be a faradiddle."

"Yes, but neither of us fell violently head over heels in love with a *rake*," Hugh protested indignantly.

Emily and Theo turned identical quizzical looks upon him.

"Oh, Hugh," Emily said in laughing despair. "How are you so—so—"

"So *Hugh*?" Theo supplied.

"Exactly!"

And he and Emily smiled at one another while Hugh wondered, yet again, whether the whole world had run mad around him.

They left Emily a little while later, and were scarcely five horse lengths away before her barouche once more became surrounded by admirers.

"Lady Emily is a most extraordinary lady," Theo said.

Before Hugh had time to express his warm agreement, they were being hailed. James, mounted upon a showy grey gelding which showed off the scarlet of his uniform to perfection, was bearing down on them at a speed that broke every rule of the Park. On reaching them, he almost unseated Hugh by delivering a forceful congratulatory slap to his back.

"Hugh! I thought you could no longer ride. How capital to see I was mistaken—one could almost think there was nothing wrong, seeing you like this."

Before Hugh could reply, Theo cut in. "Have you seen today's *Daily Chronicle*, Major?"

James's smile dropped as he turned to Theo. "I have, sir. Sometimes I wish those hiding behind their words would be placed in the front ranks as the enemy cavalry bears down on us."

Theo's smile was wintry. "Only sometimes? You're a more forgiving man than I."

"Have you a theory about whence the leak came?"

"For my money, from the regimental files," Theo mused, "although I would not like to venture a guess as to whom or why. There are as many motives as there are dishonest men."

Hugh stared glumly at Leander's pricked ears because Theo spoke the truth. James sighed slightly, as though he too was depressed at the thought, but then evidently something else occurred to him for he turned to Hugh with renewed enthusiasm.

"Now, Hugh—I must recruit your support. I have been speaking to Mama about this hare-brained scheme of hers for Sophia and told her it will not do. If she raises it with you, you must hold the line."

"Of course," Hugh agreed. He hadn't the first idea what James was talking about, but he had an eye to Theo. James should not raise family issues in front of him.

"I've told her to set her sights lower—there are many perfectly respectable gentlemen who will do for her far better than continuing to set her cap at Esdale," James surged on, entirely oblivious to the need for discretion. He had spent too long in the Peninsula where niceties were less observed; evidently he saw Theo as a fellow soldier and had forgotten where they were and of what they were speaking.

"Esdale is a good man," Theo put in, surprising Hugh. "And I understand from the ladies of my acquaintance that he is considered not ill-favoured."

Yet it was not Esdale who was in question here, but Sophia's lack of fortune. Hugh, realising James would likely offer up this information in the next heartbeat, decided to change the subject.

"Your gelding is a fine animal," he said to James. "He looks to have some Hanoverian Cream in him, if I am not mistaken."

"Good God, Hugh." James turned a withering look upon him. "How the devil can you call yourself a horseman when you betray such ignorance? As if I would ever have such a paltry, insipid, *docile* creature." His gelding arched his neck and pranced, snorting, as if to underline James's point. Or as if James had tightened the reins and pressed in his spurs in his indignation.

A lively conversation about horse breeding occupied them for the rest of the turn around the Park, and they parted ways with James at the gates.

"Your brother has very decided views," Theo remarked as they picked their way through the crowds of vehicles upon the streets.

Leander snorted, which saved Hugh from having to do so. "He knows his own mind," he agreed.

"It appears to be a family trait," Theo said blandly. "Ah, here we are."

They stopped outside Albany, Joseph coming forward and taking Theo's horse as he dismounted, before grasping Leander's bridle as well. Hugh dropped the reins and swung his good leg across the horse's neck, allowing himself to slide gracelessly down Leander's side. He would have lost his balance as his feet came into contact with the ground, but Theo was there, unobtrusively steadying him, his hands firm on Hugh's waist for a moment until, satisfied he was steady, he let him go. Hugh took a couple of steps, finding that his legs felt as if he had just stepped off a ship.

Theo was looking disgustedly at Joseph, who was feeding the eager horses half an apple each. "If they were children, they would grow up to become the most unruly brats known to man," he said disapprovingly.

"So you say, Colonel," Joseph said phlegmatically, as he began to lead the horses away. "So you *always* say."

"I have no idea why I keep him on," Theo said, but the laugh in his voice gave him away.

Chapter Eleven

By the time they reached Theo's sitting room, Hugh's leg was beginning to ache damnably. He sat beside the fire, hoping the warmth would have restored it by the time they were due to go out again. For go out they would—Theo was merely trying to decide precisely what they would do with their evening.

"We could always look in at Cribb's, or there is the Great Match at Horse Guards, though I suspect we have both spent long enough there of late."

"Great Match?" Hugh asked.

Theo pivoted on his heel and looked at him in amazement. "You don't know? How can you not know? Do you not speak to *anyone*?"

"Of course I do."

"Let me guess—Courtenay, and Colonel Badham when you have to, and perhaps Colonel Dalrymple when you receive your instructions or pass him your completed work. And then you return home, to ready yourself for an exciting night at some stifling assembly or ball. Am I correct?"

Hugh shrugged very slightly, for it was true. All of it.

"It's not precisely an exciting existence, Hugh, especially not for one used to campaigning overseas. Does it really satisfy you?"

Unlike Courtenay's comments, which were always tinged with malice, Theo sounded simply curious. It gave Hugh the courage to answer him honestly. "It used to," he said, holding Theo's gaze. "But not now."

Theo's eyes grew dark as he stared at him, and recognising the intensity in them, Hugh found himself moistening his lips. That was how Theo had looked last night. Suddenly Theo was there in front of him, and Hugh fumbled his way to his feet so he might touch him. But his leg spasmed violently and he sank back down with a bitten-off cry.

Theo instantly knelt beside him, his hand lightly on Hugh's thigh. "What is it?" he asked. "What can I do?"

"Nothing," Hugh said tightly. "Wait for it to pass." And hope to God it *would* pass because he had not had an episode this bad in months, the usual deep ache transformed into something that clawed savagely through him.

"Damn it," Theo said. He got to his feet and poured a glass of brandy for Hugh. "Drink that down and we will try again. If I can take off your breeches, then I may be able to help."

Hugh choked on the mouthful of brandy he had just taken.

"Not in *that* way," Theo said, laughing. "Have I really corrupted you so much already, Hugh?"

"It would appear so," Hugh managed, once he'd recovered the ability to breathe.

"All of it," Theo said.

Hugh obediently drained the glass as Theo crouched next to him again and began to stroke Hugh's leg with careful, warm hands. His ministrations eased the very worst of it, or perhaps the brandy was beginning to take effect. Whichever was the case, with Theo's support Hugh was finally able to get to his feet. It still hurt damnably, but he was at least mobile.

Throwing pride to the wind, Hugh took Theo's offered arm on the slow, painful journey to his bedchamber. Theo swiftly undressed him, but it was very different from the previous night—this time his concentration appeared to be on how best to remove Hugh's clothes rather than what lay beneath them.

He instructed Hugh to lie upon his front on the bed while he lit the newly laid fire.

"The room will soon warm," he said, closing the door to the bedchamber. "Now, have you heard of Medical Gymnastics?"

Hugh had not.

"When I was in Gothenberg with the Rifles, back in '08, I almost went out of my head with boredom for they would not let the men disembark for two months, which kept the officers also confined to the ship. I did, however, slip ashore just often enough to preserve my sanity, and I met a very accommodating young gentleman who taught me much about the human body."

"Did you indeed?" Hugh muttered into the counterpane beneath him. If he sounded sulky, that was because his leg hurt like blazes and not because of the existence of an accommodating young Swedish gentleman.

"I did," Theo said, and the smile in his voice came through loud and clear. "Among the things I learned was how certain procedures can relieve pain."

Hugh turned to look at Theo and found he was picking up a bottle from a small collection of such items on the dressing table. "I may have refined the technique a little," he explained, as he came over to the bed. "I find the judicious application of oil makes everything so much easier. Head down again, Hugh, and try to relax."

Hugh laid his head back on his folded arms, only to jolt in reaction as cold liquid drizzled onto his back. His involuntary movement set his leg spasming, and pain spiralled through him, tearing at him so badly he could scarcely breathe. He was panting with it, trying to control his reaction when all he wanted was to curse and cry out as Theo's hands moved in long, slow sweeps on his back, distributing the oil as they went. While the pain did not abate, Theo's touch somehow helped him to regulate his breathing, and he was thankful for it.

After a few moments of this, Theo placed his oil-slick hands on Hugh's leg. "This is going to hurt," he warned, "but it will be better after, I promise."

He was right on both counts. There was a point where Hugh was unable to keep the tears from his eyes, though he kept his face buried in his arms so Theo would never know. After the longest time, however, he became aware that something had changed—the leg that had been so outraged at the unaccustomed demands he had made of it was easing. It was no longer so tight it felt as if it vibrated with pain every time he breathed.

As the pain lessened and the room warmed, the scent of lavender from the oil filling the air, Theo's long, firm strokes seemed likely to send Hugh to sleep. He had not stopped at Hugh's leg but had administered his Gymnastic treatment everywhere, his hips, his back, even his shoulders and his arms, because the pain Hugh lived with and the awkward way in which he walked made everything tight when it should not be, Theo said. Hugh felt as if he were floating, his body freer than he could remember it ever being before, so he would not gainsay Theo's assertion.

Theo appeared to be finishing his work with long, sweeping strokes down Hugh's back, and Hugh sighed happily under his touch.

"I take it you approve of my treatment," Theo said, and he sounded amused at Hugh's open appreciation.

"God, yes," Hugh said, and wriggled slightly to underline just how much he approved.

"Perhaps you will let me know what you think of the next stage," Theo said, pouring more oil from the bottle onto his hand.

Before Hugh could wonder too much what that might be, he found out. "Oh," he said, shocked and not entirely sure what he was feeling, but almost certain he liked it.

As Theo persisted, Hugh began to move restlessly, finally pushing himself up on his arms because he could not remain still beneath Theo's touch, and Theo pressed a kiss against his spine as he continued his attentions.

"*Oh*," Hugh said again, and his head fell forward as his breath came unevenly.

Wild feelings were rushing through him suddenly, making him push down against Theo and want more so very badly. Theo knew what it was he needed, and it was not too much longer before Hugh's pleas for more, for Theo to do *something*, were answered by Theo pushing home inside him, his breathing short and harsh while Hugh's hands clenched in the counterpane, for it was both wonderful and not. And then Theo began to move, and Hugh cried out, for it was like nothing he had ever known.

By the time Theo was through with him, Hugh was a boneless, sated heap upon the bed, insensible of anything except Theo's body pressed against his. He had not known such pleasure was possible. He held on to Theo and wished they could stay like this forever.

Chapter Twelve

Hugh studied his reflection in the looking glass. He was dressed to pay a call on James in Half Moon Street, but it was not the folds of his neckcloth he was checking. He wished instead to see if he looked as different as he felt. When he was with Theo, he no longer felt like Hugh. Instead he felt like somebody different, somebody whom Theo regarded with favour and what seemed like fondness. His cheeks heated as he remembered the soft laugh Theo had given when Hugh had been writhing on his bed, completely, shamelessly, wanton, and had pressed a kiss against his temple—which had *not* been where Hugh had wanted his mouth right at that instant—before marvelling at just how responsive Hugh was to his touch. Hugh was not so surprised at that as Theo—it felt as though he had been waiting for Theo's touch his whole life.

Shaking himself from his thoughts, he set out for Half Moon Street, where he hoped to find James at home. Along the way he discovered that not only did he feel inexpressibly lighter in some unidentified way, but that Theo's treatment was still paying dividends a day after he had performed it. His entire body felt more free and less as though it were fighting his will.

On arrival at the townhouse, Matthews showed him into the morning room and brought him a glass of sherry. James burst in a few minutes later.

"Hugh! Capital! Just the fellow I wanted to see."

"Good afternoon to you too, James."

"I've been thinking, and I would count it a great favour if you would sometimes take out my horses while I am away,"

James said as he threw himself into a chair, and accepted a glass of sherry from Matthews. "They are each a bit of a handful, but nothing you could not manage, even with your difficulty."

Hugh stared at him. James's devotion to his horses was legendary. He did not simply offer them around like snuff. "Thank you, James," he said at last, deeply touched by the generosity and kindness behind his brother's offer. "I should be delighted."

"Good," James said, looking pleased.

"I wished to speak to you privately on another matter," Hugh said, as the door closed behind Matthews with a discreet click. He entered into an explanation about his concerns over open access at Horse Guards. "I know both the Life Guards and the Blues post sentries, but there is so much coming and going with the regiments, and although our offices are in another part of the building it would not be hard for somebody brazen enough to make their way there without being stopped," he concluded. "Nobody questioned Colonel Lindsay when he found his way to our office—indeed, *we* did not think to—and perhaps all it would take is somebody dressed in a uniform who carried themselves with great confidence."

James's brow had lowered progressively through Hugh's account. "I had no idea. I cannot conceive *anyone* knows how lax Horse Guards is," he said. "You make me wonder now about the War Office. I must speak with George urgently."

"Yes, but what is to be done about Horse Guards?" Hugh asked. "You know if Wellington says anything it will only be seen as another attack on their competence and they will resist."

"George," James said decisively. "He will know who to approach and how." He paused, examining the way the light reflected from his sherry as he swirled it in his glass. "Tell me, Hugh—how came Colonel Lindsay to visit you in your office? If he was awaiting an audience with the Adjutant General, it seems odd that he went wandering."

"Oh, that was boredom, I think," Hugh said with a smile, for he could not imagine how different things might have been had Theo only possessed more patience. "He had been kicking his heels for some time and was looking for a diversion. I believe it's been some time since he was last in London and so he also wished to discover from us the best places for evening entertainments."

"But how came you to be so intimate with a Rifles colonel? I know you're a reclusive fellow these days, and here you are, fast friends with a stranger within days of meeting him."

"He's easy to befriend for he is a most personable man," Hugh said, and hoped he did not blush. "I believe he was looking for company on his excursions, for he invited Courtenay to accompany him too."

"He came to two captains of whom he knew nothing for company?" James sounded incredulous.

"I imagine Lindsay's friends are all with the regiment," Hugh said stiffly, unsure whether it was Theo or Hugh that James was criticising. "You know how it is."

"Perhaps," James allowed. "I admit he had a point about the leak from regimental files. That is an entirely different thing from spying, but it speaks to the same lack of security."

"True," Hugh said glumly. "Still, I expect even that is better than a commanding officer leaking it, because poor security can be tightened but disloyalty is deadly."

"What makes you think the circular that was leaked went only to commanding officers?" James asked idly.

"That's what Lindsay said. Being a colonel, he would know, wouldn't he?" Hugh explained.

"Fair enough," James said, and he drained his glass before standing up. "I must go, Hugh—I wish to see George urgently and you know what a difficult fellow he is to get hold of these days."

As they bade one another farewell, Hugh wondered briefly about the advisability of seeing Sophia. He did not like to think of her upset, but he thought perhaps discretion was, in this case, the better part of valour. Emily had indicated in unmistakable terms that he should avoid the entire subject of Stanton and treat her quite as usual when next he saw her.

So he returned to his lodgings, and spent a quiet evening during which he did not once think about Theo spending the evening with Courtenay, which Hugh knew he had planned to do. And most of all, he did not think about Courtenay's quick brain, lively manner and attractive smile, his hazel eyes and his curly brown hair that formed an undeserving halo round his head, all of which might be enough to tempt a man that way inclined into tumbling him into bed.

Hugh didn't sleep well that night.

Hugh was working at his desk on Monday afternoon when a brief knock at the open door interrupted him. He looked up, and smiled to see Theo there.

"Gentlemen," Theo greeted them both as he came into the room.

Courtenay groaned. "I could not level the same charge at you," he protested. "No gentleman would ever treat his friend in such a shabby way as to match him bottle for bottle and then have the temerity to turn up next day looking as neat as ninepence."

"Light Bobs," Theo sighed to Hugh. "They simply cannot hold their liquor. But I am here to see if either of you has accidentally taken Colonel Badham's latest letter of instruction from the Adjutant General when you picked up regimental books from him. He is turning his office upside down in search of it, and I considered it a kindness on my part to ask you before he comes marching along the corridor and commands you at full bellow to find the damned thing."

"It is a kindness indeed," Courtenay said, "for I don't think my head could take Badham at full discharge today. But no, I have not seen anything unexpected."

Hugh had been leafing through the papers on his desk as Courtenay spoke, knowing he hadn't seen anything of the sort but looking anyway in case it had somehow got amongst his papers.

"No," he said, "at least, I do not think—oh!" As he had held the regimental book for the 42nd Highlanders by its covers and shaken it to ensure nothing was lodged in its pages, a sheet of paper had slipped out and landed on his desk. He picked it up and briefly scanned it. "Is this what you're looking for?" he asked, holding it out to Lindsay.

Lindsay's normally relaxed posture was tense as he glanced over the paper, and his hand tightened on it almost enough to cause the sheet to crumple. "It is. How long has that book been on your desk?"

Hugh thought back. "I collected it on Friday from Colonel Badham's office."

"And you have been working through it since?"

"No," Hugh said, shaking his head. "I needed it to check the accounts, but then Colonel Dalrymple wished me to deal with another matter more urgently and so I have not yet done so. I should have returned the book once I knew I wouldn't need it that day, I suppose, but I did not." Because Colonel Badham had been in an even worse mood than usual, and Hugh's leg had been hurting, and he had also been thinking more about his upcoming evening with Theo than his work.

"I shall return this to its rightful place," Theo said. "Badham will doubtless want to see you, Fanshawe. Had you but returned the book, the scare would never have happened."

"Yes, sir," Hugh said, mortified at being so upbraided, and by Theo, of all people.

Courtenay waited till Theo was well clear of the room before he looked at Hugh, eyebrows raised. "I would not believe it had I not seen it with my own eyes," he marvelled. "Captain Dutiful did not fulfil every last one of his obligations before unshackling himself from his desk for the weekend."

Hugh shrugged miserably, for what was there to say? He had no defence.

"Chin up, Fanshawe—it simply means you are human after all," Courtenay said.

Perhaps it did, but why did it have to happen in front of Theo? Hugh gritted his teeth and returned to his work. He would just have to ensure he was more careful in future.

That evening, Hugh sat alone in his lodgings. With nothing to distract him, his mind would not stop going round and round. He had endured an unpleasant interview with Colonel Badham, during which he had stood rigidly at attention for so long that his leg was now aching abominably. But none of that compared to what Theo might be thinking. He had not seen Theo again at Horse Guards, and despite his hopes, there had been no note waiting for him at his lodgings. Even if Theo was not somehow too appalled at Hugh's carelessness to wish to continue their connection, he might well have been reminded of the difference in rank between them and be uncomfortable about pursuing a friendship in light of that.

It was possible, Hugh finally admitted as he slipped on his nightshirt and climbed into his bed, that Theo had never intended to repeat the time they had together. Hugh had no guide for how these things worked. He'd hoped that they would continue to spend time with one another until Theo left for Portugal, but he had no idea what Theo's intentions had been. He snuffed out the candle and lay staring into the dark.

The next day seemed interminable. Hugh kept hoping that Theo would turn up again in their office but was disappointed, although at one point he was almost certain he saw Theo walking across the parade ground, heading away from the building. Hugh had been due to attend some gathering with his mother and Sophia that evening, but on his return home he dashed off a quick note and sent it round to Half Moon Street. Even though he knew distraction would probably be a good thing, he could not face an evening during which he had to pretend to be interested by vapid conversation.

Half an hour later, he was deeply thankful for his decision, for a note was delivered to his lodgings addressed to Captain The Honourable Hugh Fanshawe in Theo's distinctive sloping scrawl. The note expressed apologies for such short notice but cordially invited Captain Fanshawe to dinner that evening should he by some lucky chance be free of other commitments. Hugh instantly sent back a reply, stating that he would be pleased to accept the invitation.

Ascending the front steps to Albany an hour later, Hugh's emotions were mixed. He was delighted at the prospect of spending time with Theo, yet also aware of his carelessness at Horse Guards. What made his failing so very much worse was that he knew full well there was a spy on the loose and yet he still hadn't made the effort to return the book to its rightful place. He was embarrassed to face Theo again, and not entirely sure he still had Theo's good regard.

His worries were eased slightly by the smile that broke across Theo's face when he was announced. He took a seat on the sofa and accepted the glass of sherry he was given, and as the door closed behind Theo's man, he raised his eyes once more to Theo's face.

"What has you looking like a spaniel that ate the grouse it was to retrieve?" Theo asked, amused, as he rested an elbow upon the mantel and looked at Hugh.

Heat rose in Hugh's cheeks as he confessed. "My blunder at Horse Guards."

"How came you to make such a mistake?" Theo asked. "I thought you were noted for your punctiliousness."

"I believe we—*I*—have not always been careful about returning the books overnight when I knew I would need them again the next day." Although it was a habit he had picked up from Courtenay, he could not blame the other man for his failings, no more than he could blame Colonel Badham for not insisting upon the books' return. They had all fallen into bad habits, but that didn't lessen Hugh's culpability.

"But you will not do so again," Theo hazarded.

"I will not."

"Then I shouldn't refine further upon it, if I were you," Theo said. "There was no harm done as it happened, except to Colonel Badham's nerves. Now tell me, I was elsewhere today—what other great excitements have I missed at Horse Guards?"

Evidently that figure he had seen on the parade ground had not been Theo, no matter how sure he had been at the time. "The usual giddying whirl of leave requests and postings and promotions," he said. "I cannot conceive how you managed to tear yourself away from such pleasure."

"It scarcely bears contemplating," Theo agreed, seating himself beside Hugh on the sofa. "There is, however, one excitement which I missed rather more than your paperwork."

His hand rested on Hugh's thigh, and his meaning was clear. Hugh scarcely had time to fumble his sherry glass onto the side table before he was being thoroughly kissed. It didn't take him long at all to return the compliment.

It was only the prospect of dinner that persuaded them, reluctantly, to part. Not long after their meal, they were entwined on Theo's bed, soft murmurs turning to harsher sounds, until Hugh cried out with pleasure and shuddered beneath Theo's touch.

Afterward, when they were peaceful and satisfied, lying together beneath the covers, Hugh put his head against Theo's shoulder as he idly traced the lines of Theo's chest. Theo was everything he had ever wanted without realising it, and he still couldn't believe they were lying here together like this. That Theo, against all expectations, appeared to want to be with him. Theo, who was so many things that Hugh was not and could never be.

"How are you so perfect?" he asked quietly, and then realised he sounded like one of Sophia's novels and closed his eyes in mortification.

Theo pulled away and snuffed out the candles. When he lay down in the bed again, his body seemed composed of angles that had not been there before, and Hugh wished he had bitten off his tongue rather than let those words escape. Yet even in the depths of his self-flagellation, the warmth and comfort of Theo's bed had its inevitable effect, and Hugh, already drowsy with good food and wine and what had followed, found his thoughts fragmenting. He was somewhere between wakefulness and sleep when Theo put his arms around him, buried his face in Hugh's hair and sighed.

Chapter Thirteen

Hugh was relieved to find Theo was still wishful of spending time with him despite his faux pas in the bedchamber. He had invited Hugh for dinner again on Thursday night, and as Hugh left on Friday morning, he suggested they do something together on Saturday when Hugh was not required at Horse Guards.

Late Saturday morning therefore found Hugh in morning dress and impatiently awaiting a note from Theo to discover what, precisely, he had in mind. When Murray brought him a letter that had been just delivered, he was so sure it would be from Theo that he opened it without even glancing at the direction. He was surprised to find that Emily's script filled the paper.

Hugh, please come to Curzon Street as soon as you receive this. It is important *and also of the Utmost Urgency.*

All thoughts of Theo forgotten, Hugh rushed out into the street to find a hack to take him to Emily's. He had never before received such a missive from her, and he could not imagine what might be its cause.

Emily's butler showed him to the morning room before going to apprise his mistress of Hugh's arrival. Such informality reflected the easy, long-standing relationship he had with Emily, and also her thoughtfulness—she would not make him mount a flight of stairs for no reason, which he would only have to descend afterwards. But it left him waiting, and as he did so his anxiety rose still further and he began to pace the room, unable to settle the wild tangle of misgivings that chased around his head.

The door opened finally, and Emily was there. She looked to be well, there were no tears on her face, and Hugh's heart unclenched a degree.

"Hugh," she said, swiftly coming across the room and taking his hands in her own. "Thank you for coming so quickly."

"What is it?"

It did not ease his mind that she glanced around to check the door was closed before she released his hands and seated herself upon the chaise longue, very deliberately arranging her skirts around her before looking up at where he remained standing in the middle of the room. He was poised for he knew not what, unable to relax enough to sit down.

"You must promise me not to enter into a rage the instant I tell you," she said. "For we have things that must be done and cannot afford the luxury of such indulgences."

"What *is* it, Emily?" he said, foreboding seizing him.

"It's Sophia."

The blood rushed from Hugh's brain, leaving him light-headed and his heart thumping as if it were about to break from his chest.

Upon seeing his stricken expression she rushed to reassure him. "No, Hugh—it is not beyond rescue, I promise you. She is safe and unharmed."

He drew in a breath, and the world steadied once more.

"She and your mama attended Vauxhall Gardens on Wednesday evening," Emily said. "Sophia contrived to slip away from your mother, who thought she was with me. She did not reappear for almost half an hour, and at that point she came to find me, fearing to face your mama after what had happened."

"What precisely *had* happened?" Hugh asked, unable to account for the unnatural calmness of his voice.

"Stanton had prevailed upon her to walk with him along the paths, and he began to make love to her. He kissed her, and then he attempted to force further attentions upon her, at which point she became frightened and escaped in search of me."

Hugh's bottom lip was very firmly between his teeth because otherwise he would let loose words that no lady should ever hear, but it did not stop him shaking with rage.

"That *cur,*" he snarled, once he had enough control to allow words past his lips. "That damnable, Godforsaken *cur.*" He took a breath. "You say she's unharmed?"

"I swear to you, Hugh—she was frightened and upset, and now she suffers the dual burden of knowing that she was foolish and also mistaken in her trust, but that is all."

Hugh nodded brusquely. His brain was tumbling, fury clouding his clarity, yet even so he knew that he had missed something. He finally realised what it was.

"Your letter said this was urgent, but it happened on Wednesday and it has taken until now to tell me?"

Emily looked away. "Sophia assured me she was most truly sorry and would never behave in such a way again, and so I acceded to her desperate plea not to tell you."

Betrayal rose hot and sharp in him. "Emily!"

"Hugh, what good would it have done? It would have upset you when there was no undoing what had happened, and I am confident Sophia has learned a hard lesson. She fears more than anything losing your good esteem over this, for she loves you very much."

"But why are you telling me now?" The sense of foreboding had returned.

Emily sighed and looked up at him. "We thought—*I* thought—it had gone unnoticed. You know how Vauxhall Gardens is, with such a crowd everywhere, and usually those who linger on the paths are those who would not share their business publicly. But today Sophia came to see me in great distress. She attended a rout last night and there were—well, nobody said anything precisely, but she believes, as do I, that Stanton, piqued by her rejection of his advances, is letting their assignation be known."

"That *bastard.* That bloody, rapacious *bastard.*" Hugh turned away from Emily. "Forgive me, Emily, but this cannot stand."

"*Hugh.*"

At the sharpness in her voice he turned back, although his hand was already on the door handle.

"I know—believe me, I *know*—what it is you feel, but just think—if you confront him in any way at all, you give credence to what is at the moment nothing more than the faint stirring of malicious tongues. Those who know Sophia will not believe it."

"And those who don't know her? Those who saw her stand up with him, time after time? Damn it, Emily, I *told* her."

Emily got up from her seat and came to him at the door. "I know, Hugh. But you can't blame her too much. She is an innocent who fancied herself in love. He is neither of those things and knew just what he was doing. And you can't blame yourself, because short of removing her from town, there is nothing more you could have done."

"I could have stood up in the same set as them and depressed their conversation if not for this damned leg," he said furiously.

"If not for that limb, you would now be in Portugal and unable to do anything to rescue the problem we have," she said.

"Come, Hugh—sit with me and we will discuss what we must do."

Hugh sighed as he looked at her, the edge of his rage abating under her calm reasoning. Somehow he found himself resigned to being so masterfully managed.

"I am still unsure whether Julien was the luckiest man alive or simply brought to think he was," he said, and Emily laughed.

"Both. Undoubtedly both," she said as she sat down upon the sofa and waited for Hugh to join her.

The way ahead of them was clear, but they talked about it for some time. Doing so allowed Hugh to recover from his temper, and it seemed to help Emily also. Although she had no reason for guilt, it appeared Emily felt some responsibility for not having kept a closer watch on Sophia. By the time they had formulated their plans, both were calmer, perhaps buoyed by the knowledge they were able to do something. Helplessness was not something that sat well with Hugh, and he suspected the same to be true of Emily.

"Will you see her now?" Emily asked.

"Sophia is still here?"

Emily nodded. "I left her in the drawing room while we spoke. Her maid is downstairs in the kitchen, for she brought her as a chaperone."

"At least she showed that much sense, however belatedly," Hugh muttered savagely.

"Do not scold her, Hugh, *please*. She knows she was foolish."

Foolish was one word; rebellious and careless were two others. He could not promise Emily he would not scold Sophia, because how could she have been so lost to all common sense, let alone propriety? And he had *told* her about Stanton. But as Emily ushered Sophia in and he saw her pale tear-stained face, and the way her hands were clutched together, all thoughts of scolding fled.

"Sophy," he said, the old, almost forgotten childhood nickname surfacing without conscious intent. With that she was across the room and in his arms, crying against his coat as he cradled her.

"You're not hurt? He didn't hurt you?" he asked, when at last her sobs diminished.

She shook her head violently but would not look at him. "I'm sorry, Hugh," she said into his chest. "You were right, and I was utterly *stupid*, and I am so sorry."

"It's all right, Sophy." He gently disentangled himself and, taking her by the hand, led her over to the sofa. "I know you didn't mean this to happen. What we need to do now is steer a course through. Mama doesn't know, I take it?"

Sophia shuddered. "No," she said, then she stared up at him, tear-washed blue eyes imploring. "Oh, please don't tell her, Hugh. I couldn't bear it if she knew."

"She won't," he promised. "At least, not from me."

"Nor me," Emily said, seating herself on Sophia's other side. "The most important thing you must do now, Sophia, is to continue as though nothing had ever happened. Put a smile on your face and wear your prettiest gowns, and do not cut Sir Ralph, for that would give rise to speculation. But do not stand up with him again either. Your brother and I will be with you, and all will be well."

Sophia looked at Emily, and the trust in her expression almost broke Hugh's heart because he knew that despite Emily's brave words, this might not be recoverable. The Fanshawes were a perfectly respectable family, but they lacked the influence to overcome any scandal of this sort that might attach to Sophia.

"Go and wash your face and tidy your hair, Sophia, and then I will come upstairs and we shall drink some tea," Emily said. "You have a particular fondness for it, if I remember rightly."

"Yes," Sophia whispered. She looked as if tea was the last thing she wished to think about, but Hugh approved of Emily's attempt to make the afternoon unremarkable once more. She got to her feet, and then she bent and kissed first Hugh's cheek, then Emily's. "Thank you," she said, her voice strangled, before she retreated.

Emily sighed as the door closed behind her. "What are our chances, Hugh?"

He shook his head. "I don't like them overmuch, but we will do all in our power to bring this off." He reached and pressed Emily's hand. "Thank you. You are the very best of friends."

"You may repay me by accompanying me in the new high-perch phaeton I have determined to purchase," Emily said. "My groom swears he will be pitched from it and die horribly, and I begin to think he will cast himself from it if only to spite me and prove himself right." She pressed his hand in return then freed herself from his clasp and stood up.

"I think the best thing now for Sophia is for things to return to normal. Much as we both enjoy your company, Hugh, I am mindful that you do not make morning calls upon ladies, although I could bear it tolerably if you found it in yourself to do so in future. It will be best if you leave us now, and I shall ensure Sophia returns home safely in plenty of time to dress herself to promenade with me in the Park later."

Thus dismissed, Hugh found himself on the pavement and walking home mere minutes later. As he walked, rage burned bright and steady in his breast, fuelled by the helplessness he felt. He wanted nothing more than to call Stanton out, but he knew he must not.

He had just turned into Ryder Street when he became aware he was being hailed, and halted.

"Fanshawe! I was sure it was you," Theo said as he came up to him. "Yet you seemed determined to ignore me."

"My apologies," Hugh said, his response automatic and his mind not at all on what Theo was saying.

Theo looked at him, his eyes narrowed. "What is it, Hugh? What's wrong?"

Hugh shook his head for he could not tell anyone of Sophia's disgrace.

"Let me accompany you to your lodgings," Theo said, "And there you can tell me if you wish, or tell me to go to the devil if you prefer, but not before you have at least offered me suitable refreshment for I have had the most trying day already. Would you believe that Taylor has managed to mislay my favourite snuffbox, even though he swears blind he has not touched it? Short of some grubby urchin breaking into my chambers and stealing it, I cannot see how else it could have gone missing. And then there was the coffee—or rather, the drink I was served that masqueraded as such..."

Swept along by Theo's aimless chatter, Hugh found himself back in his chambers before he knew it, with Theo waving off Murray and pouring them both a drink from the decanter upon the sideboard.

"There," he said, giving the glass of sherry to Hugh, and settling himself upon the sofa. "Now will you tell me what troubles you?"

His grey eyes regarded Hugh's steadily, and Hugh knew a moment of weakness. He could trust Theo implicitly, he knew that. He also knew that Theo would understand in the way no woman ever could, not even one so excellent as Emily, the depth of his need to hold Stanton to account and the turmoil of not being able to do so.

"It's Sophia," he confessed, turning away from Theo and placing his untouched glass on the mantelpiece. "She—I regret that..." He paused, because he did not know how to say this in a way that did not reflect badly upon her. He turned back to Theo. Had he seen an iota of judgment in his face, he would have said nothing further.

"She has been inveigled into rather foolish behaviour and I believe she may be ruined." He turned away again, because he knew it was all written on his face. Sophia, so kindhearted and trusting, to be the subject of vicious slander and innuendo, and all because of that bastard.

"Who is it?" Theo was standing beside him and had cut straight to the chase. "Stanton?"

Hugh nodded. "But I cannot—oh, God, Theo, I cannot do anything to him because that would give veracity to the tale he is spreading. She allowed him to kiss her, that is all, I swear, but that is bad enough."

Theo's hand was upon his back, and though Hugh knew it did nothing to change the whole damned hideous mull they were in, it was somehow comforting.

"Will you tell me it all?" Theo asked.

So Hugh recounted the sorry tale, and at the end of it his ire was rising again. "How in God's name can I let this go?" he demanded, his hands raking through his hair in frustration. "It's a bloody thing, and he is the lowest type of bastard to bring Sophia to this."

Theo pulled him into his embrace and held him there despite Hugh's resistance. Hugh did not want some sort of false comfort. He wanted revenge, wanted action, wanted—

"Oh, God, I want to kill him," he said, and he relaxed suddenly and laid his face against Theo's shoulder. "But I cannot, Theo. I cannot."

Theo's hand was in Hugh's hair, strong fingers soothing as they stroked Hugh's scalp. "I know," he said, "and it is damnably unfair, but there are other ways."

Theo pressed a kiss to Hugh's temple, then let him go and walked back to the sideboard to pick up his drink. "What are your sister's plans for today?"

"She is to promenade in the Park with Lady Emily this afternoon. I don't know about this evening."

Theo stood considering for a moment before he tossed off the contents of his glass. "This is what we shall do. You are to tell Lady Emily and Miss Fanshawe that they will be riding in the Park this afternoon, and you and I will encounter them there. Miss Fanshawe is to wear her most fashionable habit and a smile upon her face, and all will be well."

Unlike when Emily had said it earlier, Hugh found himself believing it.

"As for Stanton, leave him to me. You're quite right, Hugh—you can do nothing without making things worse. I, on the other hand, have many options. Will you leave him to me, Hugh, and not allow your understandable desire for vengeance to lead you into anything that might cause more harm?"

It was not a rhetorical question, for Theo's gaze was fixed on Hugh's face, waiting for an answer. The very fact it took Hugh so long to furnish one made him realise that, despite knowing he should do nothing, some part of him had not yet relinquished the hope that he would find a way.

"Will you trust me on this, Hugh?"

As Theo's eyes saw into his very soul, the turmoil of rage and helplessness and shame he felt, Hugh suddenly knew. "Yes," he said, and the commotion within him began to ease. "I trust you, Theo, even with this."

Theo's smile was crooked as he turned to leave. "Don't forget to issue instructions to Lady Emily and Miss Fanshawe immediately, and I will expect you at Albany for five o'clock."

As soon as he was gone, Hugh scrawled a note to Emily. He asked her to reply immediately to let him know that she had received his instructions and to confirm whether or not Sophia was still with her and had also been apprised of the change in plans.

Once the missive was dispatched, Hugh sat back in his chair and felt as though a great weight had been lifted from his shoulders. He did not know what Theo had in mind—did not know what he *could* do—but with Theo by his side, anything seemed possible.

Chapter Fourteen

Theo and Hugh, who was mounted again on the smooth-paced Leander, had not long been at the Park when they saw Sophia and Emily entering by Stanhope Gate. Even allowing for the fact he was a brother and so might be expected to show some partiality, Hugh felt that Sophia looked extremely smart. Her habit was emerald green, which set off her copper curls, and the black military-style embroidery upon the torso and arms of her habit showed off her trim figure to the best possible advantage. The ensemble was topped off by a small black hat with gold tassels, from which a fetching green ostrich feather curled. The colour seemed to Hugh's eyes to go well with the soft brown of the habit Emily wore, which was trimmed with swansdown. Already she and Emily were attracting much attention.

Theo was riding towards them, and Hugh followed, his glare enough to scare off a couple of young gentlemen who appeared most struck by the ladies' appearance. With his usual grace and ease of address, Theo had Sophia riding beside him within moments, and it was not so long after that when her smile began to lose its forced look, until she broke into a soft peal of laughter at something he had said. Emily, riding alongside Hugh just behind them, gave him a small smile. She knew as well as he that it was not only Sophia's spirits they had to worry about, but it was still encouraging to see her transformed from the distressed figure he had seen at Emily's just a few hours previously.

Realising belatedly that any inspection Sophia was undergoing by the members of the *ton* enjoying the fashionable hour in the Park would be extended to those accompanying her, Hugh entered into conversation with Emily about her horse, who was as dainty and elegant as her rider. She also appeared to be conducting a flirtation with Leander.

"I swear there's something in the air," Emily sighed once he had brought her attention to the fact. "All we need now is for your sister to fall head over heels in love with Colonel Lindsay, and this tangle would be beyond anyone's wit to unravel."

Hugh looked quickly towards Sophia and Theo. Sophia appeared to be enjoying Theo's charming company, but there was nothing of the mooncalf about her as there had been whenever Stanton hove into view. Hugh relaxed as he realised Emily was merely roasting him.

"I think we're quite safe on that score," he said, "for Sophia has assured me that Theo—that is, Colonel Lindsay—is already in his dotage."

"I'm not entirely sure where that leaves the rest of us," Emily said, a rueful smile on her face.

At that moment, Theo held his horse back briefly. "Will you excuse us for a moment, Lady Emily, Captain Fanshawe? An acquaintance of mine has just attracted my attention, and I should like to present Miss Fanshawe."

Had it been anyone but Theo, Hugh would have demanded to know more, but it was Theo so he merely nodded in acquiescence. He and Emily watched as Theo and Sophia rode over together towards a smart barouche parked beside the track, and then Emily suddenly gasped, before laughing in delight.

"Oh, that *wretch*," she said. "Hugh, wherever did you find him? He is presenting Sophia to *Countess Lieven.*"

While Hugh knew of Countess Lieven—there was nobody in the *ton* who was not aware of the haughty wife of the Russian

Ambassador, with invitations to her soirées so highly prized—he wasn't sure why this seemed to provoke such hilarity in Emily.

"Almack's," she prompted him. "The Countess is a Patroness and able to bestow vouchers on those of whom she approves."

She certainly approved of Theo if the smile that graced the Countess's usually austere face was anything to judge by.

"Goodness, Hugh, if I were a less proper female, I might be inclined to call Colonel Lindsay a most shocking flirt," Emily said. "But as I am a proper female, I shall merely observe that there appears to be no one who is not susceptible to his charms."

"Yet you are not susceptible," Hugh ventured.

"I would mislead you if I said I did not enjoy his company," Emily said. "But you may rest assured, dear Hugh, that is all. I do, however, think he is a man of true genius. Do you see—Countess Lieven is all that is gracious towards Sophia, which means a voucher for Almack's must be forthcoming. I believe the day has been saved, for who would give any credence to the utterings of a ramshackle fellow such as Stanton when the favour of one of the most severe Patronesses shines upon Sophia? I suspect any attempt at slander from Stanton is due to his disappointment that she has rejected his suit, and so I shall let it be known if anyone says anything to me."

When Theo and Sophia rejoined them, there was a delicate colour in Sophia's cheeks and she looked slightly starry-eyed. For an instant Hugh thought Emily's statement about Sophia falling in love with Theo was true, but as she told them how gracious, how elegant, how truly *kind* Madame Lieven had been, he soon realised it was not that.

They continued along the Row, greeting acquaintances as they went, but before much longer Theo decided that they had achieved their object. Not that he put it in such crude terms, of course; instead he mentioned that they should return home in order to prepare for the evening's festivities.

"For I do not know how it is with you ladies, but I swear Hugh will take at least an hour over his toilet before venturing out, and he must be complete to a shade tonight."

Hugh stared at him. "I must?"

"Really, Hugh, you can't turn up to a ball at Spencer House in any old thing, you know. Some attention on your part is definitely required."

"You're attending a ball at Spencer House?" Sophia asked breathlessly. It saved Hugh from asking the very same question.

"As are you and Lady Emily," Theo said. "Hugh didn't you tell you? Really, he is the most hopeless brother. I should make haste and ready yourself, and Lady Fanshawe also, for she will be chaperoning you."

"I am sure she will bear up tolerably under the burden," Emily murmured, and Hugh closed his eyes briefly, imagining his mother's delight at being invited—in however roundabout a fashion—to somewhere second only to Carlton House in splendour and importance.

As Theo took his leave of Sophia, Emily took advantage of her mare's liking for Leander to lean in close to Hugh. "I do not know and cannot begin to guess how he has done such a thing," she said, her voice low. Hugh knew she had been invited to entertainments at Spencer House before now and would have more of an idea than he did the significance of what Theo had managed to contrive for them.

She moved her horse forward to bid farewell to Theo herself. "As always, Colonel, it has been a delight, and something of an education."

Theo's eyes glinted at her as he raised her gloved hand to his mouth to press a kiss upon it. "The delight is always mine,

Lady Emily," he said, with a smile that left Hugh deeply thankful that Emily had declared she had no interest there.

Theo assumed on reaching Albany that Hugh would be coming in with him, and Hugh was perfectly happy with that assumption. Once they were in the sitting room, and private, Hugh looked at Theo; he didn't know what showed in his face, but he felt almost awed by what Theo had done.

"I don't know how to thank you," he said. "It seems you have assured Sophia's good name, and at great trouble to yourself."

"Nonsense," Theo said gruffly, pouring a glass of sherry and handing it to Hugh. "I always enjoy tweaking the tail feathers of the *ton* and seeing what results. Now, Hugh, you must tell me how your leg is after our ride, for I foresee a long and arduous evening ahead of us."

"It is not so bad," Hugh said.

"Which means it is not so good either. Come along, I will have those breeches off you again."

Which he did, along with all of Hugh's other clothes, as well as all of his own. Although he began with attentions to Hugh's leg and in doing so gentled the dull ache, it did not take him long at all to turn his attention elsewhere.

Hugh was not inclined to dissuade him from that, for he wished to do for Theo what Danilo had done for him all those times. Hugh might not have Danilo's skill, although he hoped very much that he would acquire it through more practice as he found the entire experience to be just as pleasurable from this side as from the other, but Theo was evidently satisfied with his efforts, crying out Hugh's name as he spent himself. Afterwards, Theo kissed him, again and again, as though he could not get enough of him.

Eventually, however, Theo drew back from Hugh and sighed slightly. "I suppose we must make ready," he said reluctantly. "I don't know why I ever thought going out this evening was a good idea. I would far rather stay here with you."

"We don't have to stay for so very long, do we?" Hugh asked hopefully.

"Oh, Hugh," Theo said as he stood up from the bed. "You cannot leave early from Spencer House without committing a major solecism. I'm afraid we're in for a full night of it, and no mistake—Ciudad Rodrigo was a picnic compared to what this will be. Which reminds me, you are to wear your uniform tonight. This is about making Sophia's presence known, and you are not permitted to hide."

Hugh stared at Theo, nonplussed.

Theo glanced up from where he was picking up Hugh's clothes for him and placing them on a chair—a small thoughtfulness that Hugh greatly appreciated, for his leg was not well suited to bending down—and looked at him. "That's why you don't go in uniform to these things, is it not?"

Hugh shrugged slightly, not quite comfortable with realising that Theo understood him so well.

"I thought as much. So tonight, Captain Fanshawe, you will make your regiment proud. And you will wear your uniform with just as much pride as you feel for the delightful young lady that is your sister."

Hugh found himself dressed, dismissed and walking home again, all with scarcely a notion of how it had come to be. He wondered what would happen if Emily were ever to cross swords with Theo—he could not tell which of them would prevail. He swiftly decided he did not wish to know because he was not entirely sure the world would survive such a meeting.

When the Fanshawe party was admitted to Spencer House, Hugh's heart sank at what awaited him: the flights of stairs ascending from the stair hall were of a length entirely in keeping with the size of the place. Doubly thankful now for Theo's earlier attentions to his leg, Hugh took a deep breath and began his laborious ascent.

Fortunately his mother was far too taken with the grandeur of the house to find a problem with his slow pace. She seemed indeed to find it a boon, for it gave her plenty of time to enjoy the detailing of the *trompe l'oeil* balustrade to which Hugh was gripping so tightly, as well as the great Venetian lantern suspended from the vaulted ceiling, with its statuettes of naked men which, at another time, Hugh might have enjoyed. And Sophia kept an easy flow of conversation going which also managed to distract her. By the time they reached the receiving line, Hugh's bad leg was trembling slightly from the effort, but that didn't matter for there would be, according to Theo, many more hours to go before he had to descend the same stairs.

The ballroom was everything his mama's heart could have desired, and more. The grand coffered ceiling boasted a series of shallow domes and bronzed medallions shown off in the brilliant light from the many chandeliers, while extravagant displays of fresh flowers filled the air with their perfume. He left his mama—who knew better than to show too clearly her very great pleasure—with Sophia, while he began to make a circuit of the room, just in case Theo had arrived before them. Or Emily, of course. Unfortunately, his mama's eagerness meant they had arrived quite early, so Hugh ended up engaged in any number of empty conversations while he waited for Theo.

They had been there perhaps an hour before Theo was announced. Hugh looked up from where he was trapped in conversation with the Dowager Countess of Royston—he did not know if he possessed particularly bad luck or if she made a point of seizing upon him—and as he saw Theo, his breath caught in his throat.

He was used to seeing him in his Rifles uniform, which suited him as Hugh thought nothing else could. But tonight he had shed his military self and was unmistakably here as son of the Earl of Badbury. His choice of clothing was not exceptional—he had the silk waistcoat, long-tailed coat, satin knee breeches and silk stockings modelled by almost every other gentleman in the room—but he was set unmistakably apart by the way they made him look. The beautifully fitted clothes left no doubt that beneath the quiet elegance there was a very male, very strong and wonderful body. He was causing many more heads than just Hugh's to turn.

Hugh suddenly realised he was staring and returned his attention to the Dowager. Thankfully she seemed not to have noticed that she had ever lost his attention, for she was still talking of her son. Some time later, he managed to speak long enough to offer to fetch her a glass of orgeat, and she allowed him to leave. He bumped into Theo on his way. It was not, he suspected, coincidental.

Theo's eyes travelled over him appreciatively. "I can see why you do not dress in your uniform for every ball—there would likely be a riot if you did."

Hugh flushed slightly. He didn't think Theo was teasing him unkindly, but he didn't know quite how he meant it. Theo leaned in and spoke very quietly. "It is all I can do not to take you home right this instant and show you precisely what I think of you looking like that," he said, and then with a smile of the sort that one bestowed upon casual acquaintances, he moved on, leaving Hugh discomfited and slightly breathless.

He obtained the orgeat and on his return to the Dowager found she had seized upon another victim, so he was able to bestow the glass and retreat, and check upon Sophia. She was standing up for a dance with a gentleman Hugh didn't recognise, but she was smiling and his mama was watching closely so he had every confidence all was right there.

To his surprise, Hugh appeared to be much in demand despite being unable to dance. He was kept busy much of the evening ferrying drinks or escorting the occasional young lady to the punch bowl. It must have been two hours later when he stood against the wall of the brilliantly lit ballroom and finally had a few minutes peace.

"It's the curse of the scarlet coat." Theo's voice suddenly came from beside him. "The ladies can't resist it, it seems."

"I shouldn't complain if one or two of them managed to stand firm," Hugh returned, for he still had the Dowager's account of the unlikely heroics of her son Harry ringing in his ears.

"If you're speaking of whom I think you are, I have had to issue strict orders to my men not to shoot that lady's son on sight."

Hugh laughed. "I didn't think he could possibly be as insufferable as she makes him out to be."

"He's worse," Theo said promptly.

Their peace was shattered then, as Lady Spencer descended upon Theo and insisted she introduce him to somebody most desirous of making his acquaintance. Hugh girded his loins once more and began to make another round of the ballroom. This time he had a chance to talk with Emily for a moment—she had been surrounded by eager swains every time he had seen her so far tonight—and also with his mother, who could not have been more delighted with the evening because Theo had, apparently, effected an introduction for Sophia and the Marquess, and the Marquess had then stood up with Sophia for a dance.

Hugh was not sure that was such a good idea because he thought James had managed to depress his mother's unrealistic hopes for a match there. But he couldn't worry about such a little thing, not when the despair he'd felt this afternoon had been vanquished. Sophia had stood up with a number of most respectable and influential gentlemen, each of whom had appeared charmed by her pretty manners and unassuming ways. Any unsavoury gossip that Stanton might try to start was doomed before it could seize hold, for Sophia's respectability was now unassailable. And it was all thanks to Theo.

At the end of a long evening, when the guests were finally beginning to depart, he found himself saying as much to Emily. He watched Theo across the room as he was caught in conversation yet again by their hostess.

"He is the very best of men," he said, a trifle thickly, for the wine at supper had been very fine indeed.

Emily laid her hand upon his arm. "Nobody is perfect, Hugh," she said. "Not even Colonel Lindsay, difficult though that is to believe after today. You'll bid good night to your mother and Sophia for me?"

He agreed, and she went on her way. Once Sophia and his mother had joined him, Theo wandered across the room to them. "Care for a nightcap, Fanshawe? It is too early yet to retire."

So after accompanying his mama and Sophia home—and it was hard to tell which of them was more excited about the evening they had spent—he found himself at Albany yet again. It was, as Theo had said, as well that he had a spare bedchamber in which Hugh might be assumed to sleep off the results of too much drink rather than weave his way home as dawn was breaking.

Hugh had scarcely got through the door of Theo's sitting room when Theo pushed him abruptly back against the wall, his body pressed tightly against him, and his tongue thrusting between Hugh's lips. Hugh clutched at him, suddenly breathless at the feel of Theo's body plastered against him so closely, and before he could get his breath back—which was not so easy as it sounded, given the determined assault Theo was launching on his mouth—Theo drew back just enough to begin disrobing Hugh. Between dizzying, deep kisses, he murmured his appreciation for Hugh's dress uniform. His dress uniform which was, piece by piece, coming to adorn Theo's Persian carpet.

Theo's sure fingers explored every inch of Hugh's skin as he revealed it, and all Hugh could do was hold on to Theo as best he could and try to remember to breathe as Theo's slightly roughened fingertips moved over him, clever and knowing. He gasped as Theo's fingers skated across the tight, hard points on his chest, a gasp that had Theo dragging himself away from Hugh's mouth and raising his head long enough to give a smile that looked distinctly predatory, before he ran the edge of his fingernails across the same skin. Hugh groaned and hitched his hips even tighter against Theo's, desperate and wanting.

But Theo was working to his own programme and would not be rushed. His eyes were intent on Hugh's face as he unfastened Hugh's knee breeches and worked his hand inside to touch Hugh where he was already so hard. Hugh made a soft sound of desperation at the light touch that promised so much more, and Theo kissed him again, promise and need combined in the way his tongue pushed into Hugh's mouth, exploring so thoroughly it left Hugh weak and dizzy.

And then Theo's thumb stroked across the head of his yard, already wet with his need, and Hugh moaned and arched into his touch, his head thudding back against Theo's wall in a way that had Theo laughing softly as he reached his other hand up to cup Hugh's skull and bring him to rest his head against Theo's shoulder.

"I would rather you did not brain yourself until we are done, Hugh," he said. "Nursing you back to consciousness is *not* what I have in mind for you."

Despite the amusement that sounded in his voice, his eyes were dark with desire and his hand was still stroking Hugh, firm and teasing all at once. All Hugh could do was to breathe in broken little pants against Theo's neck and long for more. Theo's laughter abruptly died, and encouraging Hugh's head up, he kissed him again, a kiss that grew increasingly desperate and uncontrolled. But even then, Theo never forgot—before things had gone too far, he manoeuvred them both to the sofa, where Hugh found himself positioned in a shameless sprawl.

"For I am not entirely sure your leg would hold out, given my intentions," Theo explained, sounding so serious and calm as he knelt between Hugh's splayed thighs, before he proceeded to prove himself right. Hugh could never have stayed on his feet. Not with the way Theo's mouth felt on him, so warm and slick that he pushed up mindlessly into it, making sounds he swore had never escaped him before. Anything—*everything*—with Danilo had been a mere shadow compared to this.

When Hugh found his release with a choked-off cry, he closed his eyes, because he knew he could hide nothing from Theo in that moment.

"I've been thinking," Theo said to him later, when they were lying in bed together. Theo had once again performed his Gymnastic treatment, which had eased muscles Hugh had not even known he had. It had seemed inevitable for other things to follow, things that had left Hugh deeply content and a little drowsy.

Theo poked him in the ribs. "Are you listening to me, Fanshawe?"

"Of course," Hugh murmured sleepily, so very comfortable where he was lying pressed to Theo, holding him and being held in return.

"Good," Theo said. "I would hate to think I was wasting my profound insights on someone who was more asleep than awake."

Hugh nuzzled his cheek against Theo's shoulder, which was warm and comfortable. "Go on."

"I think it a very bad idea for you to wear your dress uniform in future," Theo declared. "It was all I could do tonight on setting eyes on you not to push you up against the nearest wall and do exactly as I wished with you. I could not answer for my actions were you to wear it again. And that, Hugh, is not a comment upon the uniform, believe me—I have no particular love for a scarlet coat. On you, however, it becomes transformed somehow. Or perhaps it transforms you—there was an air of confidence tonight that most definitely becomes you."

Hugh was vaguely aware of Theo's words, though they were softened by the cotton of sleep. He supposed idly that something had been different tonight—he had drawn fewer stares and judging looks for his limp. Perhaps when he was in uniform everyone understood what had caused it and saw the uniform rather than the weakness. Or perhaps he had concentrated so much on Theo that he had forgotten to think once of his unsoundness. And perhaps now that Theo had finally stopped speaking, he could allow himself to fall asleep because it was so very, very close and tempting...

He edged back to wakefulness for an instant as he heard Theo sigh and his arms tightened around Hugh.

"Oh, Hugh," Theo whispered. "What am I to do with you?"

But neither the question nor the unhappiness in Theo's voice made sense, so Hugh drifted back to sleep, held warm, secure and happy in Theo's embrace.

Chapter Fifteen

Hugh spent another comfortable, wonderful day with Theo on Sunday. When Monday dawned, it felt like a chore to have to report to Horse Guards. But if it were not for Horse Guards he would never have met Theo, so he should not resent so much the way it took up his time.

He had not long been back from Horse Guards that afternoon when Murray announced Major James Fanshawe. Hugh cast the newspaper he was reading to one side, surprised. James very rarely visited him in his lodgings.

"Hugh, I hope you don't mind," James started as he came in. "I was passing and thought I would drop in to see how you are. I haven't seen you much of late."

"Perhaps because you've been dancing attendance upon Miss Drury," Hugh suggested.

"Perhaps," James confessed with a scapegrace grin, as he cast himself into the nearest chair. "She is the most wonderful lady I have ever met."

"It's as well that she's the one you've proposed to, in that case. Would you care for a drink?"

James shook his head. "Thank you, no, though I hope you may be able to help me with something else. I have had the most peculiar story from Sophia and I do not know what to make of it—she tells me you and she were at Spencer House on Saturday."

"We were."

"How came you by an invitation to such an exclusive ball? Sophia mentioned something about Colonel Lindsay's involvement, but that sounds like a faradiddle to me."

"No, it's correct," Hugh said, as he thought swiftly. He could not tell James of Sophia's lapse—it would serve nothing except to further distress and embarrass her now all was mended once more. "I believe Sophia expressed a wish to attend such a thing to Lindsay, and he was most obliging."

"Obliging? I should say so. Do you have any idea—? No, I can see that you don't. But tell me, Hugh, why would Lindsay go to such lengths? Has he a *tendre* for Sophia?"

"No," Hugh said, and then realised how bald that sounded. "Not so far as I am aware, in any case. He also caused Lady Emily to be invited, as well as Mama."

"This is what I mean—this is no small thing he did, especially at such short notice. Do you not feel beholden to him now, Hugh?"

Hugh stared at James in some surprise. "No," he said honestly. Grateful, yes; beholden, never.

"I see," James said, though what it was he saw Hugh had no idea. "And forgive my curiosity, brother, but Sophia also tells me that Lindsay is on the very best of terms with Countess Lieven."

"I believe so."

"But surely he has not spent any appreciable time in London since she has been here."

"I imagine they became acquainted somewhere abroad, in that case," Hugh said. He was beginning to feel as if this was an inquisition and levered himself to his feet to pour a glass of sherry. "Are you sure you won't have one?"

"When you put it that way," James agreed, and took the filled glass with a word of thanks. As Hugh sat down, James returned to the subject Hugh hoped he would have dropped. "It is just that she is... Well. She is not precisely trustworthy, you know."

Hugh stared at him, feeling all at sea. "But she's a Patroness of *Almack's*."

James sighed. "Hugh, you really aren't the most astute of fellows, are you? She's from a German family and married to a Russian and only a Patroness because she has garnered the friendship of one or two powerful ladies whose judgment may very well be called into question. Acceptance by Society is no marker of trustworthiness, you know."

"I know," Hugh said defensively. Despite James's belief otherwise, he was not completely stupid. "But what has that to do with anything?" he asked, remembering the thrust of the conversation. "Even with what you say, our only interest in her is to obtain a voucher to Almack's, and you know how happy that will make Sophia."

"True," James said. "Though why such an insipid gathering would cause so much delight is beyond me."

Hugh choked with sudden laughter. "*Ladies* are beyond me," he confessed. "Is not one pair of York tan gloves just the same as another?"

"Well, exactly," James said, before he leaned forward warningly. "You do know that if you say such a thing in Elinor's hearing, I shall have to disown you."

"I am not entirely stupid," Hugh assured him. "I express my admiration of every single one of Sophia's gowns, even when I could swear they are almost exact copies of one another."

"Ah, but one will be trimmed with lace, you see, and another with—well, with a different sort of lace," James concluded. He drained his glass and stood up. "It's good to see you, Hugh, but I must be off. I am promised to a rout at the Drurys tonight. No, no—do not get up. I know it must be difficult for you."

He opened the door, and then turned. "Oh, by the way, have you seen anything of George lately?"

Hugh shook his head. "It must be more than a month since I last saw him, over dinner at Half Moon Street. Why?"

"No reason. I just wondered. Well, I shall see you soon, I'm sure."

As the door closed behind James, Hugh was left wondering how James always left him feeling as if he had danced with a whirlwind—out of breath from such energy and feeling just a little confused.

He leaned down awkwardly to pick up his newspaper, cursing himself for tossing it so carelessly to the floor when James had come in. As he straightened again in his chair, he wondered if Theo's latest idea might bear any fruit.

Theo had explained to him that part of Medical Gymnastics was a series of exercises designed to correct physical defects. There was nothing that could be done for Hugh's underlying problem, but Theo said there was a gentleman in Sweden who taught that the right sort of exercises, undertaken regularly, could help his mobility and flexibility. Hugh was not at all convinced such a thing was possible—if it was, why did the army surgeons not know of it?—but he was willing to try, so with Theo's encouragement, he had written a letter detailing his precise condition and symptoms. Theo had taken it and said that in the absence of a Swedish Embassy in London he would ensure it reached someone who could find out the gentleman's address and arrange for delivery of the letter. It seemed there was no one Theo didn't know and nothing he couldn't do.

Hugh wouldn't mind overmuch if the letter did not result in anything. After all, nothing could be as good as the Medical Gymnastics that Theo did with him.

When he returned home to his lodgings on Tuesday evening, Hugh was a little surprised and more than a little disappointed to find no invitation from Theo. He realised suddenly that perhaps he should be the one to offer an invitation, given the hospitality he had enjoyed at Theo's, but he also knew they were safe from discovery there. And he didn't think Theo was such a high stickler as to insist on strict etiquette. In fact, he knew he wasn't. He did, however, have a life away from Hugh and could not be expected to spend all his time with him.

Hugh decided to take advantage of not having any commitment and took himself to Half Moon Street to see Sophia. Matthews informed him that Lady Fanshawe and Miss Fanshawe had both stepped out but were expected back shortly, so Hugh elected to wait in the morning room. It was not long before a slight commotion in the hall announced the ladies' return.

"Hugh, why did you not wait for us in the drawing room? It is so much more elegant than this dreary little room," his mother greeted him as she came through the door. "Come upstairs now and tell us what you have been up to. Sophia and I have enjoyed the most charming promenade in the Park, and since the ball at Spencer House, the knocker has scarcely been quiet, you know—so many cards have been left. The Marquess was at the Park today too, and he very graciously engaged Sophia in conversation. Now come upstairs so we may speak in more comfort."

"Thank you, but this is the most fleeting of visits," Hugh said. "I merely wished to see how you both were."

"Oh," his mother said, disappointment in her voice. "Well, you must come and see us again when you have more time, Hugh. We scarcely seem to have seen you of late and I do worry about you, you know."

"Sorry, Mama," he said.

"I will leave you to catch up with your sister for I'm sure she will have much to tell you about the Marquess. He is such a distinguished man."

"Yes, Mama," Sophia murmured, and when the morning room door finally shut behind their mother, she turned eyes on Hugh that were full of laughter. "I swear, Spencer House has enlivened her in a way I have never seen," she said. "I hope your Colonel Lindsay knew what he was doing there."

"Including presenting the Marquess to you," Hugh said. "I'm sorry for that. I think Lindsay did not realise quite how determined Mama can be when she is set upon something."

"Oh, it is not so bad after all, for it turns out Lord Esdale is a most interesting gentleman. Did you know, he has such a collection of rose bushes? He is attempting to develop new ones, with different colours and scents and which are resistant to disease."

"I did not know that," Hugh said, attempting to suppress the twitching of his lips at how exciting Sophia evidently found such an undertaking.

She changed direction with a dizzying speed that reminded him of Emily. "Oh, but, Hugh, I am so glad you have come because I need—I wish..." Her voice suddenly became suspended and there were tears in her eyes.

"What is it?" he asked disturbed, moving forward. And then the composed young lady Sophia had become disappeared as his little sister wrapped her arms around his waist, laid her face against his chest and squeezed him tightly.

"Thank you," she said, her voice muffled.

"It is no matter," he said, stroking her hair and doubtless disordering a style that had taken hours to create. "I'm glad all is well. All *is* well now?"

She nodded and finally let go of him. There were still tears in her eyes, but she was smiling once more. "It is the most curious thing," she said, "but Lavinia has heard that Stanton has left London all of a sudden. Nobody seems to know why."

"That is curious indeed," Hugh said, and wondered just what magic Theo possessed.

He left shortly thereafter and was delighted to find upon his return to Ryder Street a note from Theo inviting him to dinner the following evening. Hugh felt that a letter of acceptance was scarcely necessary, but he penned one anyway, and found he was smiling as he did so.

As soon as he arrived at Horse Guards on Wednesday, Hugh felt that something was going on. There was an unusual hum of activity, and everyone who strode the corridors appeared to be doing so urgently. Colonel Dalrymple dropped at least double the usual amount of paperwork on him and Courtenay with a terse request that it all be finished that day. As Hugh stared somewhat hopelessly at the mounds of paper before him, Courtenay leaned in his direction.

"Do you think Wellington's about to move?" he asked quietly.

"Perhaps." Hugh had no more idea than Courtenay on that, but he could not think what else could cause the air of urgency and barely stifled excitement that permeated even as far as their quiet office.

"I should like to know why, when we are miles from any battle, we appear about to be buried anyway," Courtenay complained, pushing at the teetering piles of papers on his desk.

Sudden anger burned in Hugh at Courtenay's careless remark, and he turned his attention to his own papers to hide his reaction. Early in their acquaintance, Courtenay had confessed without a shred of shame that when his father had insisted upon buying a commission in the 52nd for his younger son, his favourite and influential uncle, Sir Charles Grenville, had stepped in to ensure Courtenay was assigned to Horse Guards, where the greatest danger he would face would be expiring from an excess of tedium. He had never seen action. He had never had to bury friends after a battle, nor had to see the gallant men—on both sides—who were tumbled into holes in the ground and left there. Hugh took a deep breath to steady himself, then started to read through Colonel Dalrymple's requirements.

The volume of work meant he left Horse Guards later than usual that afternoon, and when he left, Courtenay was still, most unusually, hard at work. Hugh thought about offering to help, but as Courtenay had managed to disappear part of the way through the afternoon and come back smelling of smoke and drink, as if he had visited a tavern or a coffeehouse, he decided against it. Instead, Hugh walked round to Half Moon Street, for his mother's strictures on not making himself a stranger were still ringing in his ears. He also wanted to be quite happy in his mind that all was still well with Sophia.

He stayed for a couple of hours, during which time he was regaled with his mama's activities in minute detail and able to see that Sophia appeared to be quite her old self once more. At the point his mama was about to give him an exhaustive rendition of the visit she had made to the milliners that morning, Hugh decided discretion had much to recommend it and retreated, apologetically explaining that he had another commitment.

He had not long returned to Ryder Street and was about to get changed for another pleasant evening with Theo when there came a pounding on the front door of his lodgings. Moments later, James pushed past a ruffled-looking Murray into the sitting room and closed the door in his face.

"James, really," Hugh remonstrated, standing and moving towards James.

"No, you must hear this, Hugh. We have at last caught our spy!"

"Oh, that is capital news," Hugh said warmly. "Was he at the War Office?"

It was all James could do to contain his mirth at Hugh's question. "Don't be so stupid, Hugh—it's Theo Lindsay!"

Hugh shook his head, his ears ringing. He must have misheard, misunderstood. "What did you say?"

"Lindsay was arrested an hour ago for murder and treason."

"Theo? For murder? Treason?"

"For God's sake, Hugh, stop parroting me in such a fashion. You sound half-witted."

Hugh's knees threatened to buckle, and he took a stumbling few steps and sank down in the nearest chair. "I don't understand," he said to James. "How can this be? It's nonsense—why has it been allowed to happen?"

"Nonsense?" James demanded, his air of excitement and pleasure quite vanished at Hugh's unsatisfactory reaction. "*You* are the one talking nonsense, Hugh—it was *you* who put us on to Lindsay in the first place."

"*What?*" Hugh's mouth was so dry he could scarcely get the word out.

"Telling us about how he came and went at will, and honestly, Hugh, befriending you and Courtenay like that? Courtenay is a niffynaffy fellow, and you, well... A man of Lindsay's reputation and address must have had ulterior motives."

There was such a rushing in Hugh's ears he could scarcely hear James's words as his brother plunged on. "Then that whole farrago of nonsense over the missing memorandum and Lindsay being the one to find it? That did not seem suspicious to you?"

"But *I* was the one—"

James continued, disregarding Hugh entirely. "And he has some most unsavoury contacts, not to mention expending such energies to ensure you felt indebted to him and would doubtless do whatever seemingly harmless thing he wished. Come, Hugh—you were the perfect target, with George at the War Office and me on Wellington's Staff and you being, well, *you.* I daresay he could have asked you for Wellington's plan of attack and because he wore a uniform you would have thought nothing of it!"

"*James.*" Hugh had meant it in anger, but it came out sounding despairing. "I would not—I would never—but Theo did not, *would* not—God, this is all a terrible, terrible mistake."

"Perhaps you would care to inform Colonel Badham of that. Once we have buried him, that is. For it was he whom Lindsay spitted upon a knife, leaving him to die in his own office. We can only think Badham discovered him searching his papers and had to be disposed of."

"But why do you think it was *Theo*?" God alive, would James never give him a straight answer?

"Oh, as to that, fellow obviously had his pocket ripped in the struggle with Badham, for they found his snuffbox hidden beneath the desk where it had fallen out of sight. But the net was already tightening around him, Hugh—this was simply the final nail in the coffin." James laughed suddenly. "Bit of a shame that it turned out to be a literal one for poor old Badham."

Hugh raised a hand to his head. He felt fevered, as though in the very worst sort of dream from which he would shortly wake, doubtless to find himself back in the hospital in

Salamanca, for he had not had such vivid dreams since then. "I don't understand," he said. "This is *Theo.*"

"And that's why I came to see you, Hugh, to tell you personally, for you have been rather too friendly with someone who is clearly a spy and a traitor. You must take great care to be above reproach from now on. People will allow you to have been bamboozled because they know you are, well, *you*, but you must be on your guard from now on. Any sign of liking for Lindsay, or any suggestion you might allow such a situation to happen again, and you could be in grave trouble. Do you understand me, Hugh?"

Hugh nodded mutely.

"Good. Oh, and you are not to tell a *soul* of this—we can't have word getting back to the French that we have taken Lindsay. It may be that we can get out of him who his contacts are and feed them false information. The only people to know are the generals at Horse Guards and Dalrymple, who found Badham's body."

"How is it you know?"

"Because I'm the one who went to the Adjutant General with my suspicions about Lindsay, after consulting George. The AG called me in for interview just minutes ago to inform me of what had happened. So far as you are concerned, Lindsay has presumably returned to his regiment and didn't bother telling you or Courtenay because you were merely casual acquaintances. Now, Hugh, I must be going—I am promised to Elinor tonight and she doesn't like it above half if I'm late."

"James, *please*," and Hugh could not care that he was begging, desperation so clear in his voice, because it made James turn back from where he was already opening the door. "Surely the Adjutant General does not agree with your assessment of Colonel Lindsay?"

James laughed. "Oh, Hugh, you slow-top—the AG is the one who told *me* they've got the right man. There's no doubt about it, you know."

Hugh was vaguely aware of James's departure, but it seemed as if he were in a dream. This couldn't be happening. It was madness. So desperate were they to find the spy that they seized upon the man least likely to be one, just so they could say they had done their duty. But it would all be all right in the end because Theo would prove his innocence at the court martial.

Unless, if they were indeed so sure of his guilt as James indicated, they would not listen to him.

The room spun around Hugh as he thought of it, of Theo brought up before them and sentenced to die because they would not hear him. They had no evidence to speak of but still they'd arrested him, so why would they listen to anything Theo had to say? They must. They *had* to. Hugh too would tell them they had it wrong, so very badly wrong, and surely they would listen to *him*, with George and James for brothers.

Bile rose suddenly in his throat as James's words came back to him—it was Hugh's words that had cast suspicion on Theo in the first place. It was Hugh's wretched stupidity that could cost Theo his good name and his life.

Hugh sat in his chair as the fire died, and the candles finally guttered and went out. He supposed Murray must have looked in at some point, but he was unaware of it. He sat in the creeping chill of the dark room, and as the light of dawn began to edge around the curtains, he wished to God he had died at Salamanca.

Chapter Sixteen

Sometime later, Murray appeared and asked carefully if Hugh was yet ready to shave and dress. He could not think about such frippery nonsense as neckcloths and boots and snuffboxes—

The world suddenly crashed in on him, and his heart pounded wildly.

"That's it!" He would have leaped to his feet had he not been so cold and stiff. "Murray, you are a wonder. Now quick, I must be ready for Horse Guards immediately."

He had never been so thankful for the proximity of his lodgings to the offices, for it was not much more than twenty minutes' walk, even for him. He had no idea how long he waited there, but eventually he was told by the subaltern who organised Colonel Dalrymple's diary that he would see Captain Fanshawe now.

The colonel was an imposing figure in the uniform of the King's Own Hussars, the splendour of the whiskers upon his face matched by that of the bristling eyebrows that were set above penetrating hazel eyes.

"Sir, I wish to speak to you about Colonel Lindsay."

"That's a bad business and no mistake. Have a seat, Fanshawe." The colonel got up somewhat ponderously from behind his large desk and walked around to prop his generous figure against its front. He folded his arms and looked at Hugh. "You mustn't feel too bad about being gulled," he said. "He was very good at what he did, dirty business though it is."

"But, sir, that's the thing—I have information that shows he is not guilty."

Colonel Dalrymple stood up straight all of a sudden. "Have you indeed? Tell me."

"Lindsay told me some days ago that his snuffbox was missing, that his man could not find it anywhere. He thinks it was stolen."

The colonel sighed slightly and let himself lean back against his desk once more as he inspected his boots before speaking. "And you think that somebody stole it purely in order to implicate him in a murder that had not at that point occurred and which *must* have been spur of the moment for there is no other reason to wish poor old Badham harm?"

"Yes, sir," Hugh said, but his clear certainty came out sounding a little too much like bravado in the face of the colonel's scepticism.

"How many snuffboxes does Lindsay own? How can you know if this is the same one? How can you know if he was even telling the truth—the man's a damned *spy*, Fanshawe. Even if he was telling the truth, what is to say he had not since recovered the box and neglected to inform you of such a minor event?"

"Yes, sir, but it should be entered into the record because it is relevant." It also spoke to Theo's innocence, but Hugh could see that didn't matter to the colonel—he already believed Theo guilty.

"I shall see your account is brought to the right ears," Dalrymple said, beginning to stand up. "If that is all, Fanshawe?"

"Actually, sir, it is not," Hugh said firmly, causing those eyebrows to raise in surprise before the colonel settled back down on the desk.

"There are two more things: firstly, Major Fanshawe gave me to understand that Colonel Lindsay was suspected because he was the one who retrieved Colonel Badham's missing memorandum. But, sir, that was not Lindsay—it was me." He swallowed despite himself. "Colonel Lindsay merely came into our office to ask if either of us had seen it. I found it tucked inside one of the regimental books that I had neglected to return to Colonel Badham the previous Friday evening as I should have done."

"And Lindsay asked you to give it to him, did he not? Your other point?"

Hugh moistened his lips and squared his shoulders. "Colonel Lindsay would not do such a thing, sir," he said, holding Dalrymple's gaze. "He has fought against the French, he has been injured when doing so, and he is a truly honourable man. He would not, sir, engage in such business as espionage. It is not in his character."

The colonel cleared his throat gruffly as he got to his feet and walked back around the desk to lower himself into his seat. He steepled his hands together and looked across them at Hugh from beneath those remarkable eyebrows.

"Fanshawe, I am about to give you a piece of advice that I suggest you listen to. Lindsay is as good as hanged already. If you continue on this ill-advised crusade, it is entirely possible you will join him. That would be a great pity for I believe you to be guilty of nothing more than quite remarkable naïveté and a misplaced sense of loyalty. I suggest you turn your mind to the results of Lindsay's espionage and swiftly reconsider where your loyalty lies. There are men out there who would have died if he had his way, cut down by enemy ambushes. Your men and your friends would likely be among the dead."

He finally allowed his penetrating gaze to drop from Hugh's face as he said more quietly, "You can never know what truly lies in another's heart from the words they use. Their actions are the only thing that can tell you that." After a moment's silent reflection, he looked up again. "Now, back to work, Fanshawe. As long as you do as I suggest, none of what has happened will be held against you, you have my word on that."

"Yes, sir."

Hugh groped his way blindly out of the office. By the time he reached his own desk, he was trembling. They were determined Theo was guilty. He would be hanged. Cold sweat prickled down his spine and he thought he would be sick.

"God's truth," Courtenay said when he came into the office later and found Hugh staring into thin air. "What the devil happened to you, Fanshawe? Found your way to Covent Garden at last and expired from the shock of it all?"

Hugh didn't bother responding. There was no point. There had been no point in providing evidence that might clear Theo, and there would be no point in expecting the forthcoming court martial to be fair. The result was a *fait accompli.* Theo would be hanged. Hugh looked out over the parade ground and wondered where they would do it.

He couldn't bear it. It was his fault, and it was *Theo*, and he could not allow it to happen.

He left the office, Courtenay's surprised exclamation at his sudden exit hanging in the air behind him.

James was still at home, enjoying the morning paper and a cup of coffee in the morning room in Half Moon Street. He looked surprised to see Hugh, but not unwelcoming.

"What can I do for you? Should you not be pushing sheets of paper around your desk by now?"

Hugh seated himself. "Will you tell me where Colonel Lindsay is being held?" he asked. "I should like to see him and tell him what I think of his perfidy."

"Quite right," James approved. "I shall make enquiries for you."

"Do you know when the court martial is to take place?"

James shrugged and returned his attention to his paper. "Were he not Badbury's son, I should say today, but there is bound to be some political interference. Perhaps in a few days' time."

"Will you find that out for me too, please, James? I wish to know, for I have been, however unwittingly, involved in what he has done."

"Of course," James said. Then he looked over the top of his paper at Hugh. "I expect this has all been a bit of a shock to you, but don't worry, Hugh—it will be over soon."

"You'll let me know today?"

"You may be sure of it," James promised, buried once more in his paper.

Hugh was fairly certain his brother didn't notice him leave.

Murray disguised any surprise he felt at his master's uncharacteristic return to his lodgings before the morning was over. He brought Hugh a cup of coffee, then left him in peace in the sitting room while he made himself busy elsewhere.

Hugh was thankful that he was of the orderly mind and habit that tended to attract such amused comment from others, for it did not take him many minutes at all to calculate the amount of his funds he could access immediately, and what he would have to write off as lost to him. He enjoyed a most comfortable competence, which, together with his army pay, meant he had been able to put a good deal of money aside over the years when he had been in the Peninsula and his needs were few.

The next thing he did was proceed to Hatchards book shop, his heart twisting painfully in his chest as he neared Albany. He purchased a copy of Cary's *New and Correct English Atlas*, which the bookseller assured him contained the most accurate and up-to-date maps of the country.

He spent several hours studying the maps, committing routes to memory, until he heard James's voice in the hall. He swiftly closed the atlas, placing on top of it a copy of *Henry V* he had left lying on the desk for that purpose. By the time James entered, Hugh was industriously scribing a letter of invitation to Emily.

"You have had me running about all over, Hugh," James complained as he came into the room. "I have found out what you were asking, at great personal inconvenience, I might add."

"It is very kind of you," Hugh said, getting to his feet and inviting James to take a seat.

"No, I can't stay, but I didn't wish to commit this to writing. Lindsay is due to be tried next Monday. His father is insisting on some sort of representation, can you believe? One would think he would wish to be rid of the stain on his family's honour as swiftly as possible rather than drag it out."

Hugh felt he could breathe again. That was time enough for what he had in mind. "Do you know where he's being held?"

"As to that, I can't believe you had to come to me to ask—he's at Horse Guards! Honestly, Hugh, sometimes I wonder if you were dropped on your head as an infant."

"I didn't hear anything about him at Horse Guards," Hugh started.

"Well, of course you didn't. Did I not tell you it is all being kept secret? Yet again his father has pulled strings—I can't tell precisely who he knows, but it's evidently someone with influence—and they have moved him from the Blues' guard room to a set of living quarters on the upper floor, overlooking Whitehall. God knows why he is being shown such favour, for a traitor is still a traitor, no matter his rank."

So much for a presumption of innocence until all the evidence was in and weighed. James's words were confirmation, had confirmation been necessary, of Hugh's belief that his course of action was the only one possible.

"Thank you, James," he said, and shook his surprised brother's hand. "It is very good of you to go to such trouble for me."

"Nonsense," James said. "I shall see you anon, Hugh."

As Hugh watched him leave, James's scarlet coat suddenly blurred in his sight as he realised it would probably be the last time he saw him.

Chapter Seventeen

It was shortly after seven that evening when Hugh set off for Horse Guards. He thought that was late enough to ensure he was unlikely to encounter any of his colleagues, yet not late enough to attract notice.

He had never paid a great deal of attention to the layout of the building, something he now regretted, but he was aware there existed a set of chambers on the upper floor, which a previous commander-in-chief had ordered to be created in case he ever wished to use them. Theo being incarcerated there made his plan much simpler for, unlike the Blues' guard room, the rooms were private. One staircase led to them from the part of the building containing the administrative offices where Hugh worked and another private staircase led to them from the stables.

He walked idly across the tiltyard and through the archway to the rear of the building, in the manner of one who was merely taking some fresh air after a day spent poring over dusty books. As he passed the stables he saw there was a bored-looking sentry on duty by the door to the staircase.

Hugh made his way back into the building and climbed the stairs, finding his way along the corridors until he reached a last short flight, which led to another locked wooden door with another sentry outside. Hugh had his story clear in his head—he had James's tacit permission for this visit, and while James was not posted to Horse Guards and was merely a major in an infantry regiment, he was on Wellington's Personal Staff. Hugh was confident that fact would carry huge weight with any soldier.

As it turned out, after watching Hugh's ascent of the stone stairs with scarcely a flicker of interest, the sentry did not even question Hugh's announcement that he was there to see the prisoner. He merely gave something that approximated to a salute before unlocking the door for Hugh. Hugh, surprised and relieved, remembered what James had said about Theo's arrest being kept so secret. It was unlikely that the sentries set to guard him had any idea either who he was or what he was charged with. They probably thought he was some officer who had propositioned the Military Secretary's wife or some such minor thing. Still, had this fellow been one of Hugh's men, he would have had his ears for such an incurious attitude, for he could not believe standing orders were to admit any and every visitor who might happen along.

Concerns about the continued appalling security fled from his mind when he stepped into the room, the guard pulling the door closed and locking it behind him. Hugh wasn't entirely sure what he had expected to find behind the door, for while it was a set of chambers it was also serving as a prison, but the dark wood wainscoting, crimson curtains and a painting of the Duke of Marlborough's triumph at Blenheim were definitely not in line with his ill-formed assumptions. There was also a desk and chair set by the window and a large bed in the far corner of the room.

The light from the generous number of candles flickered at the draught caused by his entry, sending shadows chasing over the figure standing in the middle of the room and briefly hiding Theo's expression from him. Theo was in his shirtsleeves, wearing the dark green pantaloons of his uniform and boots that were not quite so immaculately polished as Hugh was used to seeing on him. He was paler than usual, and there was a dark bruise across his left cheekbone. Hugh took in all of that in an instant, and then he saw the wariness in Theo's grey eyes as he regarded Hugh.

"This is something of a surprise, Captain Fanshawe."

Hugh's immediate impulse to pull Theo close, to know he truly was there and was safe, at least for now, was stifled by Theo's odd manner.

"I brought you a newspaper," he said instead, awkwardly, removing the copy of *The Times* from beneath his arm and placing it on the desk. "I was not sure if you would have been provided with one or not."

"They do seem to be a little stuffy about the civilised things in life when it comes to prisoners," Theo said. "Most odd, really."

The matter-of-fact way in which Theo referred to himself as a prisoner felt like a knife to Hugh's heart. "Theo," he choked out. "Oh, God. I'm so sorry. I swear I never meant for this to happen."

Theo looked completely bewildered, but at least he looked more like the Theo who Hugh knew, not the distant, guarded one who had been looking at him a moment ago.

"What are you talking about?" he asked. "How is this anything to do with you?"

"It's James," Hugh said miserably. "Well, it's not James, for it's my fault, all of it, but I told him how poor our security was and mentioned that no one had questioned you in your comings and goings, but it was only to show him where the problem lay. And then he got this maggot in his head about what you did for Sophia when you were only being kind, and he went to the Adjutant General and told him all. Now you have been arrested when you are entirely innocent, and it is all because of my stupidity."

"Oh, Hugh," Theo said, and he was Theo again, looking almost as though he might laugh. "I do not think the Adjutant General dances to Major Fanshawe's tune. Your brother's accounting may not have done me any favours, but I would scarcely have been arrested for procuring invitations to a ball for some friends. Were they to do that, the prisons would be overflowing."

"But—"

"No buts, Hugh. There is something else going on here, and you've done no damage, I promise you."

The crushing weight and pain that had seized Hugh's chest ever since he had heard the news eased very slightly. He drew in a shaky breath.

"Oh, Hugh," Theo said, and he sounded fond. "Have you been...? Yes, of course you have, because that is who you are." He gestured towards the chair at the desk. "But where are my manners? Please, be seated, and tell me how your sister does. She seemed to cause quite a stir at the Spencers on Saturday."

"No," Hugh blurted out.

"No?" Theo's eyebrows raised. "Forgive me, Hugh, but I believe myself perfectly well equipped to judge a social success when I witness one."

"No, I mean you will not do this. We must talk."

"We are talking, are we not? At least, *I* appear to be. Your contributions so far have been a little lacking but I wasn't going to mention that."

"*Theo.*" Hugh glared at him. "You know damned well what I mean and I will not let you divert me. We must talk, and I need—" He suddenly recalled himself and glanced at the door he had come through, lowering his voice, "I need to tell you what we will do."

"Do you indeed? Well, in that case I must not stop you," Theo said. "Please, carry on."

So Hugh told him in a low voice of the plan, how he would subdue the guard and come for Theo on Saturday, just before dawn when the streets would be almost empty of any who might recognise them, and how they would make their way out of London. "But we must not head for the ports, because those are the first places they will look. They will expect us to make for the South Coast, I am sure, because it's closest, but we can't go there in any case because it is also most heavily guarded, due to Napoleon. We should head north, but not by the Great North Road because of the tollgates. There are many other routes, less direct but safer for that very reason—nobody who might encounter us would know for sure where we are heading. I have a copy of Cary's *New and Correct English Atlas*—"

"But of course you have," Theo murmured. He was leaning back against the desk and regarding Hugh with a mixture of amusement and wonder.

"Be serious, Theo, for God's sake. I have looked and there are routes we can choose where we will never end up boxed in. With the free traders so active along the North Yorkshire coastline, we can buy passage to the Low Countries, or in the very worst case we can buy a boat. Selling the horses would help pay for it."

"You're selling my horses now?"

"We can't take them with us," Hugh snapped, exasperated. "Theo, why must you turn everything into a jest? It's your neck, for God's sake! This is the only way."

"You don't think I will prove myself innocent?"

"No." Hugh's tone was final. "They believe you to be guilty and they refuse to see the truth. I told Dalrymple about your snuffbox, I told him it was not in your character to engage in such business, but he wouldn't believe me. The Adjutant General too is convinced. You are condemned before you set foot in the court martial room. They will see you dead."

"So you come up with this wondrous, wild, *madcap* scheme to break me out so that you may spend the rest of your life as a penniless fugitive?"

"Not entirely penniless," Hugh muttered, because Theo sounded a little too much like James did when he made fun of him. "I shall make withdrawals."

"What of your family?"

Hugh swallowed. "George and James have enough credit with those who matter that it will not affect them overmuch. There will be a scandal, I know, but it will be forgotten in time, and Emily will see to it that Sophia and Mama are not harmed too badly by it, I'm sure." His voice was raw by the time he finished speaking, and his eyes stung. He would not do such a thing to them for the world, but he had no other choice. They would be hurt and it would be his fault, but if he did not do this, Theo would die.

Theo's head dropped forward and he stared at his boots for a time before he looked back up at Hugh, unwontedly serious. "Hugh—"

"I *cannot*," Hugh said suddenly, fiercely. "God, Theo, they will see you *dead* and I *cannot*."

Theo stepped swiftly forward and pulled Hugh into his arms.

Hugh buried his face against Theo's neck, feeling the powerful, fast pulse that beat there, refusing to consider that it might soon be stopped. He clutched at Theo's shirt. "I will not let it happen."

Theo let out a long, somewhat unsteady breath, and then a small laugh. "How do you do this to me, Hugh? For *you* of all people to come up with such a plan, throwing over everything you hold dear."

"They will kill you," Hugh whispered against his skin, and closed his eyes to keep back the tears that would have fallen.

Theo pressed his mouth close against Hugh's ear. "I have powerful friends," he said, his voice very quiet. "All will be well, Hugh—I promise you."

"You can't know that," Hugh protested.

"I can, and I do. I can say no more, Hugh, but I promise you, what you fear will not come to pass." He drew back then, and looked Hugh full in the face. "You cannot—you *must* not—follow this path you have decided upon. You will ruin yourself, and for nothing, you understand? It is not necessary."

"But what if—"

"Here is what we will do: every night, at seven o'clock, I will close the curtains at the window. If you see them open past seven one night, you will know all has not gone as I expect and we shall do as you suggest, although I do draw the line at selling my horses."

Hugh slowly nodded. He was not so convinced as Theo that all would be well, and he worried that Theo would only realise things were hopeless when it was already too late. He could, however, see the difficulties inherent in rescuing someone who did not wish to be rescued.

"Oh, Hugh." Theo pulled him close again, sighing as he did so. "What a damnable mess I have got myself into."

Hugh thought that Theo had something of a talent for understatement. But the mess they were in seemed not to matter so very much right at this moment, not when he was being held by Theo like this, feeling the steady beat of his heart through the shirt he wore, the strength of his arms as he held Hugh, and the warmth of his back beneath Hugh's hands. Theo's arms tightened yet further round him for an instant, and then he let him go and stepped back, leaving Hugh bereft.

"I think perhaps you should go," Theo said. "I don't know what tales you told in order to see me, but I cannot think your visit was sanctioned by those with the proper authority and I don't wish to draw attention down on you." The suggestion of a smile tugged at his lips. "There is also the fact that if you stay I am likely to forget all sense and lay you down upon the bed."

For a wild instant, Hugh was disappointed that Theo was employing such self-control, but then he returned to his senses.

Theo was watching him, heat suddenly in his gaze. "Do you have the least notion of how you look when you command me to do something? I had not seen that in you before tonight, and I confess I should like to see more of it."

"It's all very well giving you commands," Hugh protested indignantly, "but you won't do as I say."

"Oh, there are circumstances in which I would most definitely do just as you say," Theo said, and the tone of his voice and the look in his eyes had Hugh feeling uncomfortably warm all of a sudden.

"You must go, Hugh," Theo said, and he was abruptly serious. "Do not do a single thing you would not usually do. Stay watchful, and stay safe. Do nothing to draw attention to yourself, and above all, do nothing about this idea of yours to go to Yorkshire. We will plan it together if it is necessary. Now go, before I forget myself and refuse to let you leave."

When Hugh knocked upon the door to have it unlocked again, it took a few moments for the sentry to respond. When finally he did so, he looked dazed and heavy-eyed, as if he had just woken from a restful nap. Through the outrage Hugh felt at such a dereliction of duty, he reminded himself that poor security at the moment was their friend and so said nothing beyond wishing the man a good evening.

He descended the stairs, his mind slightly relieved by Theo's confidence that all would be well, although Hugh could not really believe it. Among all other indications, it had not been lost on him that Theo's court martial was scheduled for a Monday. It was quite likely, Hugh thought, that the day had been chosen in the expectation the verdict would be guilty, so that his sentence would be carried out on the very same day. The army did like to be orderly and keep its executions to a Monday where possible.

What friends could possibly be powerful enough to combat a charge of treason? Hugh thought Theo must be deluding himself, and he determined to continue his quiet preparations in case they needed to flee. He would behave as he had promised and not do anything that might look suspicious, but no one would know if he were to spend time working out precisely what they would need to take with them and learning the network of minor roads that could take them north from London.

As he left Horse Guards, he could not forgo one final glance back at the building. The curtains at Theo's window were closed tightly, giving no hint of what lay inside as Hugh set his face for home.

Chapter Eighteen

That night Hugh dreamed of a court martial where he was to speak on Theo's behalf. He stood before the court, but no matter how hard he tried to say something, the words would not come, and Theo was condemned. As they took Theo out to execute him, James laughed and teased Hugh for being such a slow-top, for if he had only found his tongue, Lindsay would have been saved. But it was the look on Theo's face as he was marched past Hugh in chains, the look of betrayal and bone-deep disappointment that had Hugh sitting bolt upright in bed, gasping.

He could not face trying to sleep again, so he spent the rest of the night reading the *Atlas* before reporting to Horse Guards earlier than usual. He couldn't help glancing up at Theo's window before he entered the building, but the only thing to see was that the curtains had been drawn back.

Remembering Theo's words about conducting himself as usual, he asked to see Colonel Dalrymple in order to account and apologise for his unusual absence the previous day.

The colonel's eyes were uncomfortably penetrating as Hugh made his apology, explaining that he had been unwell.

"I thought as much," he said. "I take it you're fully recovered and wishful to make up for your absence?"

"Yes, sir."

He left the colonel's office with a great pile of papers. Whatever had caused the air of excitement that had been so apparent just the other day was now translated into reams of paperwork, all of which was suddenly urgent.

It seemed the atmosphere had affected even Courtenay, for he wandered in a little earlier than usual. He gave a great start when he saw Hugh at his desk.

"Fanshawe, as I live and breathe! I hadn't expected to see you again—I had numbered you with the deserters, the speed with which you disappeared yesterday."

"My apologies. I was unwell," Hugh returned through teeth that were only very slightly clenched.

"An excess of sobriety, I suspect," Courtenay said. "Will you join me tonight to remedy that, for it seems my usual companion has deserted me?"

"Thank you, but—"

"You have another engagement," Courtenay finished ruefully. "It is my bad luck for sharing an office with such a popular fellow, I can see."

Hugh kept his head down and continued working. Some days he did not mind Courtenay—occasionally, he was amusing—but at other times the words that came out of his mouth were entirely mean-spirited. He had neither the patience nor the will to put up with it today. The part of his mind that was not concentrating on his work was taken up completely with Theo. He wondered if they were questioning him—James's words about getting information out of him had raised some alarming images—and how the arrangements for the court martial were progressing. More than anything, he wondered why, if Theo had such powerful friends, they hadn't yet moved on his behalf and freed him.

"God *damn* it," he swore, as his quill tip splintered under the unusual force he had applied, ugly blobs of ink splattering over the paper to mar his neat list. "*Christ!*"

"Really, Fanshawe, have a care. My tender ears, you know."

Hugh snatched up the pounce pot and attempted to rescue his memorandum, even though he knew it was a lost cause. It was that or tell Courtenay precisely what he could do with his ears, and quite possibly demonstrate it.

He gave up on the memorandum finally, took a new pen from his desk and got ready to begin all over again. As he was about to dip the quill into the ink, the pointed clearing of a throat caused him to look up. Most unusually, Courtenay had made the effort of getting to his feet and walking over to Hugh's desk, where he was now standing, looking unlike his usual mocking self.

"Is everything all right, Fanshawe?" he asked.

For one terrible moment, Hugh felt his throat tighten at such kindness because everything was very, very far from all right. Theo was still under arrest and God knew what was happening to him in this very building.

"Thank you," he managed. "I think perhaps I am not quite recovered from yesterday's illness."

"If there's anything I can do, short of taking on your work for you, you must let me know," Courtenay said, and returned to his desk. Hugh was left feeling both grateful and ashamed, for he had written off Courtenay as a lazy, selfish trifler who found spitefulness to be amusing. While he couldn't in all conscience discard that judgment entirely, there was evidently more to him than that.

He reminded himself of that when he was still working hard some hours later and Courtenay pushed back his chair and yawned. "Really, I have achieved today more than enough for an entire month," he announced to the room at large. "I must call it a day before I turn into the very worst sort of dull fellow, always chained to his desk due to some hare-brained notion of duty. Tell me, Fanshawe, what does duty have to do with paperwork? On second thoughts, please don't tell me—I think I would likely expire from boredom." He got to his feet, leaving the messy heaps of papers that characterised his desk. "Are you sure you won't join me? Lindsay has left me hanging, which I suppose is no more than one might expect from the Rifles."

Hugh attempted to hide the jolt that ran through him at the mention of Theo's name and then bit down on the anger that rose at Courtenay's careless denigration. If he only knew the truth, he wouldn't joke about Theo's sudden absence.

"I am promised elsewhere," he said, "but I'm sure you will manage to find some congenial company."

"Of that I have not the slightest doubt," Courtenay said with a knowing smile, before strolling out of the office.

Hugh stayed later than usual that evening. He told himself it was because he wished to make up for the work he had missed the previous day, but he knew the real reason—in some way, he would feel he was betraying Theo if he were to go, leaving him alone. He finally put aside his papers at almost seven o'clock and struggled to his feet, finding that his leg was stiff from the length of time he had been sitting still.

The great clock of Horse Guards, the most accurate timepiece in London, was striking the hour when he exited the building. Hugh refused to look up at it, for the mark on the dial that recorded the hour of King Charles's execution was too terrible a reminder of the danger in which Theo stood. He looked instead towards Theo's window and found he could breathe more easily as he saw the curtains had been closed.

Hugh headed for home and spent the evening putting his affairs in order. There were any number of things he needed to make sure were taken care of if he was to disappear. The opprobrium that would attach to his family once he was known to have freed a so-called spy would be regret enough for him to bear; he would not leave things so that his servants might be suspected of complicity, nor leave them without sufficient funds to pay their wages for a time. He also worked out in detail what he and Theo would need to take with them, while not loading the horses so much that they looked suspicious to anyone who marked their passing on a country road. He would need to take both his greatcoat and his Benjamin, for Theo would have no coat with him and the spring nights would be cold.

Planning and detail were areas in which Hugh excelled, as even James and Courtenay would have to allow. By the time he retired to his bed in the early hours of Saturday morning, Hugh was ready. He hoped that his plan would not be necessary, but as Saturday dawned while he lay awake in his bed, he found he could not share in Theo's belief that all would be well. The court martial was due to be held on Monday, and still there was no sign of these supposed friends of Theo's putting things right. Theo put too much trust in others, Hugh thought. It was an admirable quality in general, but not when the stakes were so high.

On Saturday evening, Hugh attended the Drurys' ball. Had it been any other commitment, he would have cried off, but knowing that the Drurys were holding this to celebrate their daughter's engagement to James, it would have been churlish and ill-mannered in the extreme to have accepted an invitation weeks ago and then neglect to put in an appearance.

In the throes of an emotion he could not name, he decided to dress for one last time in his uniform. He knew what would be said of him after tomorrow night. He would have no further right to the uniform he had tried so hard to honour, in the service of which he had become crippled. He knew that if he were to hear the tale of another soldier who had behaved in such a way, without knowing the truth—that Theo was innocent and that the court martial would be only a sham—then he would heartily condemn that man for betraying the uniform, whatever his previous actions might have been. But tonight, he still had this right.

He was late arriving at Half Moon Street, due to the fact he had walked in entirely the wrong direction at first because he wished to check one last time on Theo's window. The curtains had been closed when he had walked past at seven that evening—they had been open every time during the day that Hugh had happened past—and he knew he was probably being foolish, but he wished to be sure. The curtains were still closed—he had to assume that all was well with Theo.

Thankfully his choice of attire prevented his mother from scolding him too much for his tardiness, and by the time they arrived at the Drurys, where they were welcomed with genuine warmth, he appeared to have been entirely forgiven. By his mother, at any rate. Emily was another matter.

"Really, Hugh," she greeted him with a disappointed tone when she arrived half an hour later to find him standing against one of the walls, watching James and Miss Drury smiling at one another as they danced. "I had thought better of you. You are being dashed unsporting."

Hugh roused from his thoughts, which had not been particularly happy ones, to stare at Emily in confusion. He had no idea what he had done to earn her ire.

"Your uniform," she explained. "How is poor Mr Ivory supposed to compete with that?"

"Mr who?" he asked, more lost than ever.

"Miss Williams' would-be suitor," she said. "Really, Hugh—do you not see *anything* that happens around you?"

"It would seem not," he said, a weight settling in his chest.

Emily looked at him sharply. "In a moment you will tell me how I may help with what is troubling you, but first you must make your bow to Miss Williams, although you will be a little distracted and not speak to her for very long at all. Then you will speak to Mr Ivory and find him a most charming and amusing fellow."

Thus organised, Hugh did as he was bidden, noticing with some bemusement the wave of colour that washed up Miss Williams' face as he approached her. It was not hard to be a little distracted when speaking to her, and he soon excused himself. Mr Ivory turned out to be a pleasant enough young fellow, who appeared somewhat awed by Hugh's military record and very pleased to make his acquaintance. Mr Ivory was, however, not entirely concentrating upon their conversation, for after Hugh had left Miss Williams, another young gentleman had been introduced to her. Hugh took pity on Mr Ivory and released him quickly so he might fight his corner.

"That was well done of you," Emily approved, appearing by his side as if from nowhere. "Now, will you sit with me and tell me what is troubling you?"

Hugh shook his head, for he could not. Emily knew him too well and saw too much. "It's nothing," he said. "Tell me, how is Sophia?"

He could not ask what he really meant, in case they were overheard, but Emily understood immediately. "Very well indeed," she said warmly. "Indeed, I had no idea that your sister possessed such an interest in horticulture as she has lately displayed."

"She—what?" Hugh's head was beginning to hurt as he struggled to understand, and a wave of sudden misery broke over him.

"Oh, Hugh, you are definitely out of sorts tonight." Emily put her hand to his arm very briefly. "Perhaps a game of cards might better suit you, where you do not have to talk and pretend to be happy when you are not."

He took her advice, and the evening was made more tolerable by the company of gentlemen whose only interest was in the cards they held.

By the time he was finally free to return to his lodgings, Hugh's headache was well and truly set in, and his heart was heavy. Yet when he walked back to Horse Guards, to check one last time, and found Theo's curtains still closed with no hint of light escaping, he was filled with renewed determination and a sense of purpose. There was only one course of action possible.

Chapter Nineteen

Hugh awoke to find Sunday already well under way beneath clear blue skies. Despite the sunshine, a fresh breeze was obviously blowing—as he took a cup of coffee by the window, he saw a gentleman's hat bowling along, its red-faced owner chasing it. He was still smiling slightly as he turned away to reckon precisely how many hours he had and what he had to do in that time.

He put down his coffee cup when Murray entered the room, bearing a letter for him that had been delivered only moments before. When he saw the seal on the letter, his heart stopped, then began to pound so fast he could scarcely breathe. The seal was a design with which he was intimately familiar, for it was on the signet ring that was never absent from Theo's left hand.

Hugh's hands were shaking as he broke the seal, panic running through him that somehow he was too late, that Theo was being moved to another prison, that they had brought forward the date of the court martial, anything except what it was he read—Theo was free. He was free and back at Albany and wishful to see Hugh at his earliest possible convenience.

Hugh had no recollection of how he got to Albany, nor of knocking on the door. He was aware of nothing until the moment he stepped into the sitting room and saw Theo standing there.

"Oh, God," he said, and it was wrenched from him. "*Theo.*"

He was vaguely aware of the door being closed behind him as he crossed the room as swiftly as his leg would allow and pulled Theo into his arms, unable to contain his joy.

"God," he said, "Theo," as he pressed kisses to his face and his lips, because Theo was here. He was alive. He was safe.

He must have taken Theo by surprise with the force of his reaction, for it was an instant before his arms came around Hugh, and then he let out a great sigh and held him so close that Hugh felt as though their hearts were beating together.

"Are you truly cleared?" Hugh asked at last. He knew it must be so, but he had to be sure.

"I am," Theo said. He pulled away from Hugh's hold, gently at first then disentangling himself more abruptly when Hugh would not immediately let him go. "I must talk to you," he said, and his voice was like his body had suddenly become, full of hard angles.

Hugh stared at him, not understanding, and Theo turned away. He walked over to the empty fireplace and propped one booted foot on the fireguard.

"I've been released because the real spy has been identified," he informed the marble mantelpiece. "It's Courtenay, but he appears to have got wind of his discovery and is nowhere to be found."

"Courtenay? *Captain* Courtenay?"

"The same."

It seemed impossible to Hugh. *Courtenay?* "Are you sure they have it right this time?" he demanded. "They were convinced it was you when that was evidently nonsensical. I can't believe Courtenay, of all people—"

"I'm sure," Theo interrupted him. He looked up and held Hugh's eyes, and his gaze was hard. "The French are in possession of misleading information that I gave only to him. There can be no doubt."

All of a sudden Hugh felt every inch the slow-top that James so often accused him of being. "How—you—" he started, but he couldn't find the words he needed, so he settled for the simple plaintive truth. "I don't understand."

"Wellington knew there was a leak at Horse Guards. He was certain who it was not, but there were unknown quantities, particularly among the more junior officers. I agreed to investigate."

"So when you went drinking with Courtenay, you were really..." Hugh's voice died. He stared at Theo, who would not hold his gaze and looked back into the empty grate. "Both of us," Hugh said. "You suspected both of us and that's why you befriended me."

"Yes."

Everything seemed sharp and clear suddenly, as it all fell into place like the tumblers of a lock. "You fed us both false information and waited to see which version reached the French."

"I did."

It was like being in the Pyrenees again, with the air so thin and the room so cold as the truth slowly took root in Hugh. Theo's friendship had only ever been a simulation, created to deceive him. The happiness Hugh thought he had found with Theo had never existed.

"I see," Hugh said, and his voice did not sound like his own. He made a futile attempt to gather any remaining shreds of dignity around himself. "You have done an exceptional job, Colonel Lindsay, and as an Englishman I must thank you for your devotion to duty, no matter how unpleasant it must have been."

He turned to leave, knowing that his voice had splintered at the end and betrayed him.

"Hugh," Theo said, sharply, almost desperately.

Hugh stopped, but he would not, could not, turn around. He didn't know what more Theo could possibly have to say.

"When I took you to my bed, it was not part of this," he said.

Hugh's eyes closed briefly. He didn't know why Theo would lie now, about this. He turned to challenge him. "Yet you still talked of regiments and routes."

"I wanted to believe you innocent, Hugh, but there was too much at stake. My instinct told me you were exactly as you seemed, but I had to be sure I wasn't simply telling myself what I wanted to believe. I had to be sure." His eyes were intent on Hugh's face. "Do you understand?"

Hugh certainly did understand. Theo had taken Hugh to his bed so he might either prove himself innocent or give himself away.

Giving himself away was precisely what he had done, Hugh realised with a rush of shame. He had responded with such wretched eagerness to every advance or attention Theo had bestowed upon him. As for the scheme he had dreamed up when Theo was arrested…

"Why the charade about being arrested?" Why pile yet more humiliation on to Hugh? He had betrayed himself completely in that upper floor room, clinging to Theo and practically confessing his love for the man. He wished desperately for the floor to open, or the heavens to fall, or anything to happen that he would not have to remember what he had done.

"Being arrested was not part of my plan, believe me," Theo said ruefully. "I admit Courtenay took me by surprise there. He knew that once Horse Guards believed they had caught their spy, he would be safer and could go about his business unhindered. Having had to dispose of Badham, he found the perfect opportunity to frame me."

"The snuffbox that went missing," Hugh started, for it was easier to think about the mechanics of the situation than about anything else.

"That was stolen," Theo corrected, "when Courtenay searched my chambers. Nothing I had said or done could lead him to suspect me, so I believe he merely suffered from an excess of caution. Perhaps that is why he seized upon the snuffbox, to have it for a contingency. Or perhaps he simply wished to ensure that if an intruder was detected, he would be thought to be no more than a common thief." Theo smiled suddenly, though there was no humour in it. "As it happened, once I was arrested he became positively careless and fell into the trap set, passing false information about Wellington's plans for an assault next month. Once he had done that, he was to have been seized, while I was released with no blemish on my name." Theo's smile changed, until he looked genuinely amused as he added, "And thankfully no pressing need to sell my horses or visit the Godforsaken county of Yorkshire."

Hugh stood as tall and straight as his leg would allow. "Am I to be arrested for treason?"

All colour fled from Theo's face as he stared at Hugh. "Why would you say such a thing?"

"Yorkshire," Hugh got out, his voice thick.

"God, Hugh, *no. Never*, I swear. That was between us, that was—no, God, do not tell a soul," Theo pleaded, his eyes dark with something that if he did not now know better, Hugh would have thought to be distress. "It goes to the grave with me."

Hugh supposed numbly that he should be thankful for that, though he could not guess at Theo's motivation. No more than he could guess at the reasons for any other thing that had happened.

"How did that memorandum come to be in the book on my desk?" he asked.

"I can only think that Courtenay took it to make a copy and then could not find a way to replace it without risk of discovery. Hiding it in the book meant it could look accidental, or it could cast suspicion on you." Theo shrugged slightly. "Either way worked to his advantage."

"Did it cast suspicion on me?"

A slight smile touched Theo's lips. "It assured me that I was right. No one who was guilty could have reacted in the artless way you appear to have perfected as your own."

"I see," Hugh said. He was fighting hard to sound like Theo, matter-of-fact and untouched by this, but it felt like Salamanca all over again—one moment striding forward, certain and sound, and the next the ground cut from beneath his feet, and so much pain. "So that's when you knew I was innocent?"

Theo shook his head impatiently. "I knew—I *believed* before then, Hugh," he said. "But I had no evidence. And until I came to know you, you were the perfect candidate: quiet to the point of invisibility, at Horse Guards for long hours each day, with your brothers placed as they were and your unexpected friendship with Lady Emily, who was until lately married to a Frenchman."

"You suspected *Emily*?" Horror almost choked him at the situation Emily might have found herself in. "God, man, have you no shame? How could you ever think that of her?"

"You forget, I didn't know her. Nor you. And there was always the possibility you were being milked for information while remaining innocent."

Hugh looked down, shame and anger filling him. "You think me so stupid?"

"No! God above, *no*. But when you trust, it seems you trust wholeheartedly, and you do not expect to be betrayed."

"It's true," Hugh said quietly, looking back up to find Theo's eyes were intent on his face. "I did not expect it from you."

Theo took in a sudden sharp breath. His face was wintry, his lips thin and tight.

"I wish you good day," Hugh said, and turned to leave.

"Hugh," Theo said.

But there was nothing left to say. Nothing to be done except to get out of this place and attempt to forget all about Colonel Theo Lindsay. It appeared Theo also realised that, for he said nothing further as Hugh opened the door and left.

The walk back to his lodgings was a peculiar kind of torture, because Hugh's leg meant he could not hurry. He could not get away from where he might be seen or greeted by someone he knew, and the sunshine that had been so bright with hope as he had hastened to Theo's now taunted him. Finally he was through the door and safely into the familiar rooms that were dark after the day outside. He went to his bedchamber, for it was the only room with a lock, and he could not have anyone see him, not even Murray. Not yet.

He sat on the bed and saw with surprise that his hands were trembling. He supposed he should not have been so shocked by Theo's revelation. The very concept that a man like Theo Lindsay could have an interest in Hugh was ridiculous. Hugh had always known that but had elected to ignore it, instead behaving like a spoiled child who believed he could order the world as he wished it to be instead of how it really was. He'd chosen to believe he, *Hugh*, could somehow earn the regard of such a man, and he had no right to be surprised when the entire edifice he'd constructed came tumbling down around his ears, for it had never had any foundation.

Hugh buried his face in his hands. God, he had been so stupid. So terribly, monumentally stupid, and the worst of it was that Theo knew it. Theo knew everything about Hugh's wretched delusions and infatuation.

When he'd been with Theo, everything had seemed different and anything had felt possible. But nothing had changed—he was still Hugh, still the stupid third son who had gone to war and come back too damaged to be of any use.

He hated Theo Lindsay then, with everything that was in him, because he had made Hugh believe, if only for a short while, that things could be different.

Chapter Twenty

That night Hugh slept very ill indeed. The brandy he had consumed to help him sleep brought him only bad dreams. As a consequence, he was out of bed several hours before he was due at Horse Guards, desperately seeking a diversion, but there was nothing he could do that would rid his mind of thoughts of Theo and his own damnable stupidity. When finally Murray appeared to start the day, Hugh practically fell upon his neck in gratitude. With his usual morning routine begun, things grew easier, for Hugh could concentrate on the minutiae, and he knew that at Horse Guards he could lose himself for the day in paperwork.

It was only as he left his lodgings to walk to Horse Guards that it occurred to him to wonder if Theo might be there today. He missed his step and stumbled. No, of course he would not be—what possible business could he have there now? Even if he *were* there for some reason, he would not come near their office, that was certain.

Relieved, Hugh continued on his way. After he had gone another twenty paces or so he suddenly realised it was no longer "their" office. He had been so taken up with Theo's revelation that he had not really thought about Courtenay. He hoped he was caught soon—he would not wish a hanging on any man, but Courtenay's actions were unpardonable. It might have seemed a game to him, as removed from the war as he was, but his actions had belied that when he murdered Colonel Badham. Then he had tried to frame Theo, who was entirely innocent of murder, if not of other things. And from what Theo had said, Courtenay had not thought twice about pointing the finger of suspicion at Hugh, no matter the sentence that would be passed if he were found guilty. No, Courtenay deserved the fate that would be his.

The office felt different as he entered, and he swiftly realised it was not only due to his knowledge that the other occupant would never be there again, but the fact that every last scrap of paper was missing from both of their desks. He stood for a moment, unsure what to do. The sound of a throat being cleared behind him caused him to turn around. Colonel Dalrymple's subaltern was standing there, looking distinctly awkward.

"The colonel wishes to see you, Captain Fanshawe," he said. His message delivered, he scuttled off.

Colonel Dalrymple possessed considerably more ease of address than his junior, but the same air of awkwardness pervaded his office as Hugh entered, closing the door behind him as bidden.

"Take a seat, Fanshawe," he said somewhat over-heartily. "I take it you've heard about Courtenay?"

"Yes, sir," Hugh said as he carefully lowered himself onto one of the chairs in front of the colonel's desk.

"Shocking business. He's one of the Oxford Courtenays, you know."

"Yes, sir," Hugh said, although he had no idea what bearing that fact had on anything that had happened.

"Now, I should like you to tell me every person Courtenay has mentioned to you and every place he has mentioned frequenting, even if only once. It appears he has been very careful, but even the most careful man might slip occasionally, especially if, as I suspect to be the case here, he has underestimated his listener."

"Sir?"

"He's an arrogant young pup," the colonel said. "It would not surprise me in the least if he played games to amuse himself with his own intelligence and daring, telling you things that he would not risk mentioning in front of another because he deemed you something of a dullard."

"Yes, sir," Hugh said. His cheeks were hot with shame.

"It was his blunder," Dalrymple said, his eyes very steady on Hugh's face from beneath bristling eyebrows, "mistaking steadiness of purpose and a sense of duty for dullness. So let us see if we may hoist him with his own petard, Fanshawe. Tell me everything."

Hugh trawled through his memories, bringing to mind odd snippets—the dark-haired opera dancer, Arabella, the names of the hells Courtenay had said he had frequented and the occasional fellow he had mentioned encountering there, even if only to complain about their bad habits with dice or cards.

"Excellent," the colonel said when at last Hugh was finished, and he looked with satisfaction at the list of names and places on the paper before him. "That will be of great value, Fanshawe—thank you."

Hugh nodded and hoped the colonel was right.

Colonel Dalrymple cleared his throat, and suddenly the sense of awkwardness was back. "There is one further thing," he said, and his voice was gruff. "While there is no question attached to you, not even the merest hint of a stain upon your character, I regret that the generals wish anybody who was associated with Courtenay to be cleared out as a precaution."

Hugh's stomach turned, and it was suddenly hard to breathe. The colonel could not mean…

"I'm sorry to say that you're being moved to half-pay and are no longer required at Horse Guards," the colonel said quickly, and he was looking at the paper in front of him as he said it.

"Sir," Hugh said, and then fell silent, for he did not know what to say.

The only sound in the room was the ticking of a clock, and Hugh's breathing, faster than usual and uneven with panic.

"Look, Fanshawe, it's a damned mess," the colonel said suddenly, looking up and straight at Hugh. "They've made the wrong decision in this case and so I have informed them, in no uncertain terms. Colonel Lindsay also made most forceful representation, but they refuse to budge." His shoulders rose briefly in an apologetic shrug. "Perhaps it's not entirely a bad thing, for you can go to Bath and try the cure for that damned leg of yours. I know it troubles you. And as soon as the frenzy dies down, I will be requesting your return because I have never before had a man as careful in his work as you."

"Thank you, sir," Hugh said between numb lips. It was not only his lips—his entire body was numb. He did not know what to do, what to say. He did not know anything except he must get up from this chair and walk out of Horse Guards and away from everything.

The colonel got to his feet and moved around the desk to lay a strong hand on Hugh's shoulder. "If you should need assistance of any sort, Fanshawe, don't hesitate to look me up," he said. "I'm damned angry they've done this to you, and so I've told them."

Hugh pushed himself to his feet. "Thank you, sir," he said again, and then he was out of the room, along the familiar corridor, and stepping into the fresh air and brightness of a day that had no business continuing as if nothing had happened.

He walked along Whitehall, though he had no idea where he was going nor why. He simply knew he had to keep moving because otherwise his emotions would overwhelm him.

He found himself at length standing beside the river, watching the wherries that plied along its waters. There was an ache deep inside him that nothing could ease. For the first time in his life, Hugh didn't know what to do. All he knew was he couldn't stay here, not when what had been his life was taken away from him and there were reminders of Theo Lindsay at every turn.

He didn't know how long he stood there, the tumult in his head so loud he could scarcely think, but he slowly became aware of the steady, soft slap of water against wooden pilings. The sound took him back to spring days splashing in the streams at Carswell. He remembered the way he and James would run home with jars full of tadpoles and Miss Nash would scold them for being muddy and wet and late before providing them with a larger container for their catch. Hugh and James would take turns in feeding them each day, watching them grow and turn into frogs, at which point Miss Nash would insist they returned them to the wild, despite James's best attempts every year to persuade her to allow them to place some of the frogs in Sophia's bed. James had not changed all that much. And suddenly Hugh knew what he would do. It would not solve anything, but it was what he needed—a safe place where he could retreat and regroup.

He looked around and found to his surprise that he had almost reached Battersea Bridge. He did not like to think for how long he must have been walking. Turning back, he headed for the Palace of Westminster, because he needed to see George.

It turned out, of course, to be impossible to see George—Lord Fanshawe was a very busy man these days—but his secretary, Mr Charles, graciously allowed Hugh to write George a note on his own stationery. He undertook to ensure George received it and that Hugh would obtain an answer as swiftly as possible. Having impressed upon him the urgency of the matter, Hugh made his way back to Whitehall and found a hack to take him home, for the pain in his leg was becoming unbearable. He had walked too far, and it was letting him know of his dereliction.

Once back in the safety of his lodgings, Hugh warned Murray they might shortly be travelling to Carswell. He could do nothing else to further his plan just in case George refused his permission for Hugh to use the estate as a refuge, so, having spoken to Murray, there was nothing for Hugh to do.

Nothing except realise that this was how the rest of his life would be now. If he could not go to Horse Guards every day, he did not know what he would do with his time, for he couldn't engage in any physical pursuits. He had never been precisely bookish; he thought now that perhaps that would have to change, else he would run mad. Or perhaps he could breed roses like the Marquess. At that, Hugh found himself laughing, and then the tears came. He ended up with his head in his hands, and wetness on his fingers that he tried to tell himself was due simply to the pain from his leg. Unfortunately, Hugh had never been a convincing liar.

Chapter Twenty-One

Mrs Mason met Hugh at the front door to Carswell, having evidently been drawn out of the house by the sound of the post chaise. It had been an easy journey as the estate was only one stage's drive away from London, but Hugh's leg was still protesting the long walk he had taken two days previously, and his dismount from the carriage was awkward. As soon as he was safely established on the ground, he smiled warmly at Mrs Mason—she was part of coming home again, having been a fixture at Carswell for all of Hugh's life. She looked suddenly older and smaller than he had remembered, and his smile dropped when he saw the tears in her eyes as she gazed at him. God, this was going to be no different from London, with the pity and distaste from everyone.

"Oh, Master *Hugh*," she burst out, twisting her hands in her skirt. "We thought... When we had the news about that terrible battle and heard you were injured, we thought we might not see you ever again, and yet here you are." Tears started to spill down her cheeks, and Hugh's heart squeezed at the mix of distress and happiness on her face.

He walked to her as swiftly as he could, and proffered his arm, drawing her hand inside the slight curve it formed. "I'm perfectly well, Mrs Mason," he said. "I promise you."

He pressed her hand in a way he hoped was comforting as he escorted her back into the house. He wished he had thought to visit Carswell before now—it had never occurred to him that anyone other than his immediate family would have cared what happened to him. He was deeply touched, yet also worried she might continue crying, because he had no idea what he should do in that case.

"I am very sorry to spring myself on you with such little notice, you know," he said, "because I realise I have put you to a great deal of trouble."

This was precisely the medicine Mrs Mason needed, for she immediately sniffed back her tears and puffed up indignantly at the very suggestion she was not at a moment's notice ready for even the Prince Regent himself, should he care to visit. Despite her words, Hugh was glad he had delayed for a day before travelling to Carswell, no matter how difficult he had found the waiting, for it had meant she and the other few servants who'd been left to ensure the place didn't go entirely to rack and ruin during the Season had had at least a little time to prepare.

After hearing all of Mrs Mason's news, Hugh partook of a cold luncheon and made the acquaintance of Mrs Mason's exceedingly tall nephew, Peter, who had been taken on as a footman since Hugh was last here. When the household had removed to London, he had remained here in order to do whatever tasks around the house were too heavy for Mrs Mason. From the muscle on the fellow, Hugh was sure he need have no worries that Mrs Mason was being overly stretched in that regard.

Once he'd eaten, Hugh headed for the stables. During the journey to Carswell, he had found idleness to be his enemy. His mind had insisted on replaying every single time he had betrayed himself to Theo by making it so evident, beyond any hope of misunderstanding, just what he had felt for the man. And his inconveniently clear memory had delighted in reminding him that even on those occasions, Theo had dropped into their conversations information about military manoeuvres, never losing sight of his goal, no matter the scorn he must have felt for Hugh. As his stomach clenched in misery, Hugh tried to walk more quickly. He desperately needed the distraction of riding or driving, something that would occupy his mind. For now he made himself consider just what cattle might still be in the stables, with most of the horses in London.

He was trying to recall every horse the family had owned over the past ten years when he reached the stableyard and Jim, the groom who had been left to run things, came out from the tack room. He seemed almost as pleased to see him as Mrs Mason had been, judging by the way he spat on the ground and muttered that it was about time because they'd almost forgotten what the captain looked like.

The equine pickings were as slim as Hugh had feared, even if slim wasn't quite the right word for the big black mare with white stockings that Jim brought in from the field and got ready for him.

Contrary to his expectations, it was not at all difficult to ask Jim for assistance with a boost into the saddle.

"It'll do that lazy mare good—mebbe run a bit of the fat off her if you make her work today," he said as he passed Hugh a whip before giving Molly a slap on the neck that was doubtless supposed to look disapproving but which instead betrayed his love for the animal. "Will you be taking her far?"

"I'd thought I'd go to up to the folly. It's been a while since I've been up there."

"We'll see you when you get back, then. And you, you great jug-headed bone-setter," he added to Molly, "you mind your manners with the captain."

Hugh laughed suddenly, surprising himself. He'd missed this, affection hidden beneath gruffness and supposed insults. It was like the regiment once more, and a fellowship he'd lost on leaving Spain.

"Don't worry," he said, waking up the dozing Molly by gathering up the reins and squeezing his right leg against her. "I'll make sure she's on best behaviour."

"Good luck with *that*," Jim grumbled as he disappeared in the direction of the tack room.

Hugh was still smiling as he got the reluctant mare to leave the stableyard behind. It was several minutes later, as he rode beneath the lime trees that lined the driveway, that he realised—Jim had, in his inimitable way, been checking on Hugh's route just in case something happened and he ended up getting thrown. Hugh wanted to feel resentful for, yet again, he was reminded that he was different now, but he couldn't. It was kindness, and it was subtly done, and if Hugh *did* come off the rather broad Molly, which he could not see happening unless he slid right round the butterball, he would simply crawl home if he had to, the same way he'd crawled off the battlefield at Salamanca, before the flames that swept across the dry grass could reach him.

The long, steep ascent to the folly, standing on top of the tallest hill in the area, slowed Molly's steps. Aware she was out of condition, Hugh was content to let her go at her own pace. Within reason, that was—he did intervene when her own pace involved snatching mouthfuls of grass as she went.

And it was worth the climb when they reached the top, for the view in all directions was splendid and far-reaching, with three counties visible on a fine day. It hadn't changed one iota from when he had been here as a boy, although he had no intention now of setting himself to rolling back down the hill the way he and James and sometimes George had done, to Miss Nash's chagrin as she had seen the mud stains and torn clothes that had inevitably resulted. He grinned suddenly. The woman had deserved a medal for putting up with them.

He chose a route back through the woods, enjoying the shade under the trees, for the day had grown warm. The familiarity was welcome and soothing. More than anything, though, the freedom of having a horse under him once more, the ability to cover distance without effort and without pain, was beyond anything he could express. He supposed, regardless of all else, he should be thankful to Theo Lindsay for giving this back to him. But as thoughts of Theo threatened to intrude on his peace, he nudged the mare into a canter, determined to leave those thoughts far behind.

Hugh didn't return to the stables until late that afternoon, and Jim was there to meet him when he did. He was not so adept as Theo at steadying Hugh on his dismount, but he was strong and steady, and that was all that was needed.

By the time Hugh had bathed and changed and eaten, he felt relaxed and more than ready to retire to his bed. He didn't know what magic was in the air at Carswell; all he knew was that he felt somehow restored. He still had no idea what he was to do with himself, but it no longer felt so desperate. He knew that somehow he would find a way through, just as he had after Salamanca.

That optimism lasted precisely as long as it took him to slide between chilled sheets and blow out the candle. For no reason he could explain, the dark seemed to press in upon him. As the silence of the house grew heavy in the darkness, Hugh felt more alone than he had ever been before. He had grown used in such a short time to lying beside Theo, to having Theo's warm body pressed against him while his arms held Hugh. He'd become used to lying upon his pillow, just looking, because he could not help marvelling at how perfect Theo was. He had become accustomed to the way Theo would look back at him, and then, so often, how looking would turn to kissing, and Theo would press Hugh backwards and lie on top of him, his body anchoring Hugh in a way he had never known he needed.

Hugh's eyes were screwed closed and his breathing ragged, because he couldn't bear it. He couldn't bear to think it had all been a deceit. And he didn't know why Theo had done it. It would have been enough for his purposes only to be friends with Hugh—he had not needed this as well. Why had he done it? He had never seemed unkind or cruel in his teasing of Hugh, but what he'd done to him was the cruellest thing possible.

Tears were pricking in Hugh's eyes as he buried his face in the pillow and tried to steady his breathing, but it hurt, it hurt too damned much to think of what Theo had done, and Hugh did not know why. What had he done to deserve such a thing?

His only answer was the silence of the dark bedchamber.

The next day Hugh took Molly out again, hoping that more exercise and fresh air would help him sleep soundly that night. When the time came for him to retire, he did indeed sleep, but he was subject to restless dreams.

When he turned up for Molly, for the third day in a row, he could have sworn she rolled her eyes at the sight of him and the prospect of yet more work. He greeted her with a slap on the neck of the sort that Jim bestowed.

"My sincere apologies, madam, but you do need to work for a living," he said, and refused to let the irony of what he had just said spoil his mood.

He took her out towards the Downs, and they came back the long way round, splashing through the ford and up the drive to the house in the late-afternoon sunshine. He could feel the effects of the length of his ride in his leg as Jim caught him upon his dismount, but despite that, Hugh felt better for the outing.

He was almost cheerful as he made his way into the house, meaning to wash and change. Peter, who appeared to have modelled himself after Matthews' admirable example, stopped him halfway across the hall. "Lady Emily d'Arcourt is in the drawing room, Captain Fanshawe. Miss Fanshawe and Miss Williams are also here, but they have gone into the gardens."

He was not entirely sure he could have heard correctly, but on entering the drawing room he found Emily sitting upon the sofa, reading a book. She glanced up as the door opened, and a smile lit her face.

"Hugh!" She placed the book on the table beside her and stood to greet him, moving towards him with her hands outstretched to catch his own in her grasp. "It is such a relief to see you, for if I had to endure one more hour of what Lord Esdale says about one thing or Mr Ivory about another, I swear I might have had to knock two young heads together."

"Emily." Hugh was still shocked. "But what are you doing here? It's lovely to see you, of course, but I was not expecting you."

"I hope you don't mind," she said, "but London was becoming tedious, and Lady Fanshawe said you were here so I conceived the notion of a change of scene, and once Sophia heard, nothing would do for her but to accompany me. Where Sophia goes, so does Lavinia these days."

As the door closed behind Peter, Hugh allowed himself to be drawn to the sofa. He sat down, with Emily settling beside him. Her smile had faded, and her eyes quartered his face. "I came because I was worried about you," she said. "It seemed to me out of all character for you to leave without saying goodbye, and I wished to reassure myself all was well with you. But it isn't, is it?"

Hugh shook his head. He could not even begin to admit all that had happened. "It's nothing," he said, a trifle thickly, for Emily's kindness had brought it crashing back.

Emily took his hand. "Hugh, the girls are chattering together in the garden and won't return for hours yet. You can tell me, if you will, for I see something is very wrong."

Even had he been able to tell her of the true nature of his friendship with Theo, Hugh knew he could never confess to

Emily the depth of his shame. But there was something else weighing on him for which he bore no fault, and he knew he would have to tell everyone sooner or later. He might as well begin now.

Even so, it took him awhile to say it, for saying it would make it real. “Horse Guards,” he said at last, his voice strained. “There was a spy, and because we shared an office, I was an inconvenient reminder of what had happened. I am no longer welcome there.”

Emily said nothing for a time, for which Hugh was grateful. Sympathy at the moment would be his undoing. “That can’t be easy, Hugh,” she said eventually.

“It’s more that I can’t see what to do now,” he confessed. “There is nothing else I *can* do.” He closed his eyes briefly, because he would not let Emily see the desperation that racked him at the magnitude of his loss.

Her hand squeezed his slightly, but before he could embarrass himself beyond all hope of reparation, she started to speak. “Well, now we are here, you can show me and Lavinia all the places Sophia has been speaking of and which she tells us we will love. I had thought tomorrow that the four of us could take a picnic to—what is the name of the lake you fell into as a small boy when trying to copy James and George by jumping across the stepping stones? Or perhaps that doesn’t narrow it down enough to identify it.”

Despite himself, despite *everything*, Hugh found himself smiling. “Sophia will catch cold at telling tales,” he said, “for as her older brother, I remember everything she did.”

“I can see this is going to be a most entertaining visit,” Emily said. “Oh, but, Hugh, I am desolate to have to inform you that Lavinia’s affections have been captured by another.”

“Thank God for that,” he muttered.

Emily ignored his shocking lack of gallantry. “It appears that when she and Sophia were walking in Green Park, Lavinia was saved from a dreadful fate at the jaws of the most fearsome beast, which was threatening to attack her. Mr Thomas Ivory appeared as if from nowhere, wrestled the terrible animal to the ground and bore it off. And with it, it appears, Miss Williams' heart.”

“I take it from your tale Miss Williams was never in serious danger,” Hugh deduced.

“Perhaps of being licked to death. It was young Annabel Trent's poodle puppy that had thought to make a new friend. Apparently Lavinia is not accustomed to dogs.”

“Well, it seems I must bow out for a better man has taken the field,” Hugh concluded in tones of great gloom.

“And that despite the splendour of your regimentals,” Emily sympathised. “I can see how you must be quite cast down. Oh, but speaking of upsets reminds me—I was in danger of displeasing your excellent housekeeper, Mrs Mason, when we arrived, for we had reservations at the inn three miles away, not wishing to overturn your household with our unexpected arrival. As well as we three, there is my maid and Sophia's maid, and then my groom refused to allow my horses to be looked after unsupervised by the ostlers at a *posting inn*—indeed, he did say it with such a horrified expression upon his face—and I could not even consider bringing such a number of us here. I regret Mrs Mason was cut to the quick by my thoughtlessness and I was only able to make it up to her by many apologies and explaining that I had not wished to overset you, knowing what an ordeal so many ladies would be for a modest gentleman such as yourself. I capped off my apologies by producing Sophia, for I believe you and she are quite Mrs Mason's favourites.”

“Sophia is, certainly,” Hugh agreed. “I fear I have never been forgiven for the time we were playing hide and seek and I hid in the linen chest. My shoes were muddy and apparently I managed to wipe them on every single piece of linen before I found a better hiding place."

"That quite throws my sins into the shade," Emily agreed. "Especially as I agreed I would immediately relinquish my foolish plan and we are to stay here."

Hugh decided he was glad of it, for when the young ladies came in from the garden they were most excited to see him, with Miss Williams blushing only a little, and they enjoyed a lively evening together. Sophia was in raptures to be back at Carswell, while Miss Williams appeared most struck by the way Lady Emily had handled the ribbons when she had taken them driving in the Park yesterday and was now desirous of learning to drive herself.

Such enthusiasm was almost overwhelming, and as he caught Emily's amused gaze across the dining table, he smiled. He had perhaps needed reminding that he had the very best of friends in her and Sophia, and the warmth of the welcome he'd received from the servants had also reminded him that his life was really not so miserable as he had begun to believe.

Mrs Mason's words came back to him, for he was fortunate to have survived Salamanca. He had much to be thankful for, and he knew it. If only he had never met Theo Lindsay, he would be content with all he had. As it was, he now wanted more, so very much more, but it was not to be. He shook himself from his thoughts and concentrated fiercely on the ladies' conversation.

Chapter Twenty-Two

The next morning, Emily's idea of a picnic was greeted with great enthusiasm by the young ladies, especially once Emily had promised to let Lavinia have a turn at the ribbons and Sophia had been assured they would return in time for her to quiz the gardener about plants to her heart's content. Hugh had turned a surprised gaze on Emily on hearing of Sophia's desire, but Emily had merely smiled.

It was a good day. Nobody fell into the lake, despite Sophia and Lavinia insisting upon going back and forth across the stepping stones; the luncheon Mrs Mason had packed into wicker baskets was delicious and plentiful; and the sunshine was warm, but not so hot that they needed to remove their chairs to the shade beneath the trees.

They made a happy party as they came back into the house, Lavinia and Sophia with their heads together, giggling over something, with Hugh and Emily following, her arm tucked comfortably into his.

"Are they always so excited?" Hugh asked, eyeing the young ladies as they divested themselves of bonnets and parasols, which they passed to the patiently waiting Peter. "And if so, for how much longer do you mean to stay?"

"Hugh! I am shocked at such boorish behaviour from one who is usually a paragon of virtue." Emily then leaned in closer to ask in a low voice, "Do you really mean I can't leave them here with you?"

As Hugh turned his horrified gaze on her, Peter cleared his throat.

"Excuse me, Captain Fanshawe," he said. "There is a visitor desirous of seeing you. He would not give his name but neither would he leave, so I was obliged to show him into the morning room. If you wish me to eject him..." The prospect quite clearly delighted him.

"No, that will be quite all right. Thank you, Peter," Hugh said, puzzled as to who it possibly could be.

"Indeed, sir." Gloomy disappointment oozed from Peter's every pore as he opened the door to the morning room.

The sun was streaming through the Venetian windows, casting the figure that stood in the centre of the room into silhouette. It took Hugh a moment to realise who it was.

"*Theo*," he blurted, thunderstruck.

"Hello, Hugh. Lady Emily." Theo made a brief bow in Emily's direction. She did not return the greeting but stared at him with narrowed eyes. "Hugh, I don't have long, but I must see you."

Hugh looked from him to Emily, who squeezed his arm before releasing it. "The girls and I will have tea in the drawing room," she decided, "leaving you and Colonel Lindsay to speak of matters military. Perhaps, Peter, you would be kind enough to ensure the gentlemen are not disturbed?"

Peter, as susceptible as any to Lady Emily's charms, was very pleased to agree he would certainly do as she had asked.

Hugh was left alone in the doorway, staring at Theo. He was dressed in a plain dark coat, buckskin breeches and top boots, and a sword hung by his side. He looked pale and strained.

"What are you doing here?" Hugh demanded, and he could not tell if it was shock or anger that made his voice unsteady.

"Close the door, Hugh, if you please," Theo said. "This is not for anyone else's ears."

Hugh came into the room and shut the door firmly behind him.

"I'm leaving for France and must catch the evening tide, hence my hurry," Theo said. "But I couldn't go, not with the way things were left between us, Hugh. I had to see you."

Hugh moistened his lips. "For what purpose?"

"I wished to apologise to you," Theo said abruptly. "Not for what I had to do—I cannot and I will not apologise for that—but for allowing other things to become enmeshed with it. I should have known better. I *did* know better, but it seemed I couldn't help it. Or I chose to believe that I couldn't. It was badly done of me."

Hugh couldn't follow all of what Theo was saying, but on that he could, and did, agree. "It was."

Theo's mouth twisted at Hugh's words, and he raked his hand through his hair, an uncharacteristic gesture that Hugh realised was designed to buy time. He was finally learning to read Theo Lindsay—he wished it had not taken him so long.

"And yet, Hugh, despite everything, I find myself hoping you might somehow be prepared to overlook my egregious behaviour. That we might perhaps..." Theo's words trailed off as Hugh stared at him, disbelief warring with anger. Surely Theo could not be suggesting they could pretend they had ever truly been friends.

"I accept your apology," Hugh said stiffly at last, when it was clear Theo would say nothing further. "There is no more to say. The entire episode is best forgotten."

"Hugh—" Theo started, and then broke off as the clock on the mantelpiece struck the hour. "Damn it to *hell*," he swore. "Hugh, I must go. Had you been but five minutes later I should have missed you completely. But would you do something for me?"

It was presumptuous of Theo to ask him for anything, but Hugh found he could not say no. Not with the way Theo was looking at him, resignation on his face as though he expected a refusal, but with a flicker of hope in his tired eyes.

"What is it?"

"Where I'm going, I can't take this with me," Theo said, and Hugh saw he was drawing his signet ring from his finger. "Will you hold it for me until I return?"

Whatever his feelings towards Theo might be—and Hugh was no longer at all sure of that, for everything was jumbled up inside—he could not refuse. It was evident Theo was engaged upon business for Wellington, and it was incumbent on Hugh to aid him in that.

He held out his hand and Theo placed the warm gold circle into his palm. Hugh found that his fingers closed swiftly and tightly around it. "I will keep it safe."

Theo's gaze rested on his face, and Hugh had no idea what the expression in his eyes meant. Then he sighed. "I must go," he said. "Time and tide will not wait even for me."

"France, you say," Hugh said, for it was only now registering fully with him. Theo's destination had not been foremost among his concerns on first seeing Theo.

"You'll say nothing until I've returned, I know."

France was enemy territory. Who knew if he *would* return.

"*Theo*," Hugh said, suddenly urgent.

Theo was already opening the door. He turned.

"Stay safe."

Theo's smile was crooked. "Always," he said.

And with that he was gone.

Chapter Twenty-Three

Hugh had no idea how much time passed while he turned Theo's ring over and over in his hand. He had never thought he would see Theo again. He had certainly never thought Theo would apologise for what he had done.

He traced the entwined initials, as elegant and strong in their lines as the man who bore the name. He had trusted Hugh with something of such value, the symbol of who he was, and Hugh couldn't understand why.

His hand closed once more around the ring when Emily came quietly into the room. "May I join you, Hugh? The girls have gone to get changed for dinner."

She waved him off when he would have stood. "Of course," he said. Truth to tell, he welcomed the distraction, for his thoughts had been going round and round and he was no closer to understanding Theo Lindsay than he had ever been.

"It was a surprise to see Colonel Lindsay," she said conversationally, sitting down beside him on the sofa.

"Yes," he said, and smiled slightly, for it had been rather more than a surprise.

"He is gone again, I see."

"Yes."

"Will he return?"

"*Yes,*" Hugh said urgently, denying instantly any other possibility. Theo would be safe in France, no matter the dangers he faced, because he must. As Emily looked strangely at him, he realised belatedly what her question had actually meant. "That is, I don't know how long he will be gone."

"But you will be seeing him again?"

Hugh nodded as his hand tightened on the gold band, for that was one thing he could now be sure of.

"I was not quite sure you were pleased to see him," Emily said casually. "All is well, I take it."

Had it been anyone else in the world, Hugh would have moved the conversation on adroitly. But it was Emily, who knew almost everything about him, whether he wished her to or not, and who would see through any pretence he attempted.

"Why would he give me his ring?" he asked her, and opened his hand to show her. "I know he can't take it with him where he is headed, but why *me*?"

Her lips parted slightly as she looked, but she did not try to touch it, for which he was thankful. His hand closed once more on it, protectively.

"Well, you're friends," she said slowly. "It's a sign of the great trust he has in you." She hesitated, looking at him. "If he has offended against you in some way, perhaps it is his way of ensuring you will see him again, for you will need to return it to him."

He stared at her. "Why should you think Theo has offended against me?"

"Perhaps I am wrong, but there was something in the way you looked when you saw him, and in his expression as he regarded you. And it is true that even such men as Colonel Lindsay can sometimes make mistakes." She leaned in closer and added, "Although if I find he has indeed done something that has vexed you, I shall not swiftly forgive him, you may believe me."

His smile at her was somewhat sentimental. Emily was, as her brother had been, the very best friend Hugh could have wished for.

She stood and shook out her skirts. “I suppose I too must change for dinner. We mustn’t let the young ladies outshine us, Captain Fanshawe.”

Much later, Hugh lay in bed, looking at Theo’s ring where he had placed it next to the candlestick. He was thinking about what Colonel Dalrymple had said, about it being a person’s actions rather than their words which showed their true intent. Hugh had not fully understood all that Theo had said to him that afternoon, and he still did not understand Theo’s reasoning for leaving his ring with him, but he knew it meant *something.*

It was clear that Theo regretted what he’d done. Hugh supposed he should be glad to know that, but he would rather Theo had stayed away completely. Seeing Theo again had brought it all back, the pain of the betrayal and the humiliation he felt. Seeing Theo had also reawakened all sorts of yearnings in Hugh’s heart, which could never be realised. No, Hugh would do better to forget all about Theo Lindsay. Once he had returned his ring, he would have no need to see the man ever again.

Hugh snuffed out the candle and turned over, determined he would be able to sleep now he had come to a conclusion about the entire situation. Instead he found himself wondering again about the ring. Because it seemed Theo wished to see him again, although he had no need to, not now he had made his apology and it had been accepted. Although Hugh told himself he didn’t care to see Theo ever again, he knew he was lying. Yet what friendship could ever exist between them, with Hugh being Hugh and Theo being who he was? And with Theo knowing of

Hugh's pathetic infatuation also? Shame heated his cheeks in the darkness.

As he continued to turn restlessly in his bed, it slowly dawned on Hugh what had really been going on that afternoon. Theo had come to see Hugh in order to clear his conscience—and Hugh refused to admit the reasons a man embarked upon a dangerous endeavour might feel that need—and had left his ring with Hugh merely because it had been his last stop before he boarded whatever vessel was taking him to France. It had been nothing more than that, and Hugh had refined too much upon it.

As the clock in the hall struck three, he wondered if Theo was yet in France, stealing past the guards Napoleon must have set on the coast, or if he was still crossing the dark Channel. Hugh imagined Theo standing on deck, his only companions the riffling of waves against the hull and the creaking of ropes as he waited for the dark coastline to reveal itself, hoping he reached it before the dawn betrayed him to anyone who might be watching.

Hugh turned over again. He would not think of the risks Theo ran. But he picked up Theo's ring, and when he finally fell asleep it was clutched tightly in his hand, as though by keeping it safe he could protect Theo also.

The next day, Emily claimed Hugh for a turn around the gardens. They left Sophia and Lavinia to do whatever it was they did that involved so much giggling and whispering.

"I think it is two young ladies who are a trifle giddy because they are in love and the objects of their affections appear to return their feelings. Here they find themselves with freedom to indulge themselves," Emily explained as they walked beside the flowerbeds. "They will behave properly when we return to

London. Which, dear Hugh," she said with a squeeze to his arm, "I think we shall do tomorrow, if you do not object."

"Of course," he said. "But what do you mean, in love?"

"I think you know very well what I mean," she said, and her tone was so loaded he knew she was trying to tell him something. As so often, he wasn't sure what. "But I believe your sister, to everyone's surprise—not least her own—has discovered Lord Esdale to be a fascinating gentleman."

"She has?"

"Indeed. Now tell me, Hugh, will you return to London when we do, or do you prefer to stay here?"

He hadn't thought that far ahead, and he was silent for a while. He didn't yet feel able to face Ryder Street and the emptiness of his life there now, with no Horse Guards and no—well, there never *had* been Theo, really, and the sooner he trained himself into that way of thinking, the easier it would be.

But as his fingers slipped into his pocket to check Theo's ring was still safe, he found himself wondering all over again, because some part of him—the part that had so disastrously betrayed him before, allowing him to believe what he wanted, not what reason told him—whispered that Theo had left his ring with Hugh not merely because it was convenient.

"I think I shall follow you back shortly," he said eventually, and Emily smiled.

The ladies left the next morning. Without them the place felt blessedly peaceful. As the day wore on, however, the silence began to feel a little lonely.

Two days later, as he returned Molly to Jim after his daily ride, he found he had come to a decision. Hiding here would change nothing. It still cut deep that he was not welcome at Horse Guards, but it no longer felt like the end of everything.

The next day found Hugh heading back to London.

Chapter Twenty-Four

Hugh called in at Half Moon Street to let his mother and Sophia know of his return and found himself swept up in their plans for that evening. The Beauchamps were giving a ball and, knowing Lady Fanshawe's preferences, had included Hugh in their invitation. She had not seen fit to consult him when she had replied some time since, accepting on his behalf. Hugh scarcely had time to return to his lodgings and have dinner and change his clothes before wending his way back to Half Moon Street to accompany the ladies.

As it happened, Hugh was pleased he had made the effort to attend, for he had the chance to observe Sophia standing up with Lord Esdale. They behaved with perfect propriety, of course, but as they looked at one another, they both smiled more than was usual. Esdale was a couple of years older than Hugh and pleasant-looking enough, but with none of Stanton's dark handsomeness. Hugh wondered if Sophia had been attracted by Esdale simply because he was so different from Stanton. It worried him that she might be close to forming an attachment based purely on a reaction to a bad experience, which wouldn't last.

When Hugh was presented to the Marquess, however, he soon realised that Sophia's attraction was not necessarily only about safety and respectability. He appeared to be a straightforward and most good-natured man who possessed a certain quiet charm. He was fully informed, or at least as informed as the newspapers could render him, about the war in the Peninsula and asked Hugh his thoughts on several aspects. Hugh then ventured that he had heard the Marquess was keen on developing new types of roses, and that was when he fully realised why Sophia was as taken with the man as she was. Esdale's face lit with enthusiasm and he was full of excitement as he explained things that Hugh had never thought he would find interesting. He found himself intrigued by Esdale's detailed descriptions of his methods and aims, and even interpolated an occasional question.

"And I thought that if I combined those two, the repeat flowering of the first and the strength of the second, the result will be a strong flower that is not too showy, yet beautiful and constant. There is a purity to the way the rose will look, I feel, and it will be a forgiving plant, naturally kind."

Hugh blinked. He might not know much about roses, but he was fairly certain they weren't usually described as kind.

"Do you know what you will call the new bloom, my lord?" he asked, a suspicion striking him.

Esdale looked away, colouring slightly. "As to that, I have an idea, but it may not be my choice."

"With the care you take of your beloved plants, I can't think that you will be disappointed," Hugh said.

He was rewarded by a hopeful smile before, with an obvious effort, Esdale wrenched his mind back to conversational topics. "I understand you're friends with Lindsay," he said.

Hugh froze for an instant, conflicting emotions twisting inside him at the mention of Theo's name. "I am," he said cautiously.

"Well, can you find out what ails the man?" Esdale asked. "He appears to have gone to ground—at least, I have not seen him for days, and last week he was damned miserable. He simply avoided the subject when I raised it. You know what he's like."

Hugh nodded. He knew all too well that Theo would not allow anyone to know anything about him that he did not choose.

"It's not that I need to know, for chances are it's none of my business," Esdale went on, "but he's a good man and I don't like to see him so evidently out of sorts. Especially as he's bound for Portugal again soon, I should imagine. Your brother's heading back there shortly, I understand from Miss Fanshawe."

With that, conversation turned more general. A short time later Hugh excused himself, for the Marquess was a popular guest and much in demand. He approved wholeheartedly of Sophia's choice, although he realised his approval was neither needed, nor necessarily a good thing. His lack of judgment in these matters had been amply demonstrated by the whole mess with Theo.

The thought of Theo was an ache deep inside Hugh as he stood in the middle of the busy room, with music and laughter and conversation filling the air around him. He couldn't remember ever feeling so alone.

Over a leisurely breakfast the next morning, Hugh attacked the pile of post that had been awaiting his return. Most were invitations of one sort or another—the price of being seen as his mother's escort—but there was a bulky packet, which puzzled him until he opened it. It was a letter, several sheets thick, from the Medical Gymnastics gentleman in Sweden. Forgetting all about his bacon, he fell to studying it.

The gentleman, Mr Ling, had very awkward handwriting, but Hugh eventually got into the way of reading it, and the content was fascinating. Mr Ling explained about his theory and wrote of things that Hugh could do to help his leg, and had even drawn some diagrams to explain why these things would help. Hugh could not follow some of the more technical explanations so, after finally finishing his breakfast, he took himself to Hatchards. There he bought the first volume of *Elementa Physiologiae Corporis Humani.* He was most taken aback to learn that there were another seven volumes and assured the eager shopkeeper that one would be quite sufficient for now.

Walking back in the afternoon sunshine with his new purchase, he suddenly realised that being a gentleman of leisure might have its compensations, for he could sit and study this at will rather than have to delay his explorations until the evening. As he waited to cross the road to his lodgings, allowing plenty of space to a curricle that was being driven at far too fast a clip for the crowded street, he found himself revelling in the unaccustomed feeling that he could please himself in where he went and when.

He crossed the road, pausing for an instant as he thought he saw someone familiar moving past his lodgings, but the gentleman was walking quickly and disappeared from view among the street vendors before Hugh could place him. He realised it was unlikely any of his friends from the regiment would be back in London in any case; while all was kept secret, the change in the weather meant Wellington's next offensive would surely take place soon. In fact, it was certain to be soon if they had fed false plans to the French via Courtenay, for it meant the true plans must already be in place.

Hugh sighed slightly as he sat down at his desk. He still didn't understand what had driven Courtenay to do what he had. What could possibly lead a man to spy for another country? He knew Courtenay played deep, and had wondered if it was simply for money, but he thought it must be a character flaw more profound than that.

He wondered too about Theo. He had thought, when Theo first told him about investigating Hugh and Courtenay, that

Theo had just happened to be a trusted officer who had volunteered. His leaving in secret for France gave the lie to that, and Hugh's lips twisted as he remembered his declaration to Colonel Dalrymple that Theo did not have it in his character to engage in espionage. God, he'd been naïve. He'd never really known Theo. All he'd known had been what Theo had allowed him to see, and it turned out that none of that had been real.

But Theo had also fought at various battles in the Peninsula—his knowledge was not of the sort that came from secondhand accounts. Perhaps he was simply a Rifles officer who had a facility for passing unseen or unquestioned, and that had been taken advantage of. Although as Hugh remembered the amount of influence Theo appeared to have and the networks he utilised to assure such things as Stanton's disappearance from London, he supposed miserably that he was still being naïve.

He found himself wondering all over again when Theo would return from France. That led him to the realisation he might not return at all. Hugh refused to allow that thought to take root, instead turning his attention to the book he'd bought, because tomorrow he was going to begin the regimen of treatment that Mr Ling had suggested for him, or at least those parts he could do on his own. He was eager to see what, if any, difference it might make. Of course, it could never match up to what Theo had used to do for him. He cut off that thought immediately, because thinking about Theo caused only regret and confusion and a deep, abiding ache. He determinedly opened his book at the first page.

It was only when Murray came in to light the candles that Hugh realised he'd spent hours deep in study. It had been as if a new world had opened up to him, and he found himself with a sudden understanding of what drove Esdale with regard to his roses. Murray also brought with him a letter that had been delivered. It was from Sophia, begging his participation in a party they were making up to go to Vauxhall Gardens that evening, for there was to be "Great Entertainment", the phrase heavily underlined.

Unable to resist Sophia's excitement, he penned a quick reply before realising he had only two hours in which to change and have something to eat, for he knew the pickings at Vauxhall would be slender. With a feeling of regret, he closed his book, and then remembered that he would have all day free again tomorrow to continue his study. It appeared he was going to take some time to become accustomed to being on half-pay.

Chapter Twenty-Five

The Fanshawe party walked for a while through the pleasure gardens at Vauxhall. Both Lady Fanshawe and Sophia pronounced themselves very well pleased with the evening as they stood upon a delicate iron bridge and regarded the waterfalls, admiring the way the droplets that flew free from the cascades glistened and sparkled in the light of coloured lanterns. Yet for all their enjoyment, it did not take long for them to agree that the only thing more comfortable than this would be taking their place in their box and enjoying a light supper. It was not long before the reason for both ladies' eagerness became apparent, because among the company who joined them in the box was Lord Esdale.

Hugh partook of the supper, although the portions were scarcely enough to keep a sparrow alive, the size of the so-called chicken they were served leading him to suspect it was in fact a sparrow. The rack punch was pleasantly strong, however, and made up for the lack of food. He exerted himself to make polite conversation, but when the orchestra began to play and the fireworks started—the great entertainment of which Sophia had written so excitedly—he excused himself, after casting one final glance in his mother's direction to ensure her eye was firmly upon Sophia. Not that he could imagine Sophia would ever do such a thing again as disappear along one of the dark walks. In fact she looked as though she would never willingly move from Lord Esdale's side, listening intently as he explained something about the fireworks as they burst in bright streams of colour.

Hugh appreciated the excitement of fireworks—as a boy, he had imagined nothing could be more splendid than creating his own, which he could set off whenever he wished—but since the Peninsula, the noise brought back memories of artillery fire, of attacking across open ground and men falling around him. These days he preferred not to observe them for long.

Shaking off memories, and finding the Grand Walk a little too crowded for his liking as people gathered to stare up at the display in the sky, he took himself along one of the dark walks. There were fewer lanterns in the trees here, but those few were still brilliantly coloured. He scarcely encountered a soul along the walk—it seemed everyone had gone to where they could better see the fireworks. Such privacy suited Hugh after the evening he had spent, and he wandered peacefully, despite the loud bangs as rockets burst overhead. He could almost imagine he was in some fairyland, with the trails of glittering light across the sky from the fireworks, and the lanterns in the trees forming groups of violet and blue and red that looked like sparkling flowers caught among the branches.

A body slammed into him suddenly, sending him staggering into the hard trunk of a tree just as a particularly loud rocket exploded. Before he could get his leg back under him to fight off his attacker or recover his breath to demand what the devil was going on, a hand was across his mouth and a body was pressing him back against the tree.

"Quiet," a voice hissed, and Hugh was shocked to realise his assailant was none other than Theo.

With a heroic effort, Hugh kept obediently silent and still, seeing with confusion that there was a small pistol in Theo's hand as he watched a drunken figure staggering along the path towards them. The gentleman stopped long enough to cast up his accounts all over the roots of one of the trees before setting out on his wavering way once more, muttering to himself as he did so and looking as if he might measure his length on the grass at any time.

As he passed them and continued on his unsteady way, Hugh could feel Theo relax slightly. Once the man was lost in the distance, he slid the pistol out of sight. He released Hugh's mouth from beneath his hand, only to frame Hugh's face with his hands.

"You're safe?" he asked urgently, and his face looked almost wild in the half-light. "You're not hurt?"

Hugh, confused, shook his head. There was part of a branch jutting most uncomfortably into his back where Theo had forced him against the tree, but he didn't think that was what Theo was asking. He could not understand why Theo was here when he had thought him in France, let alone why he had set upon him in such a way and now seemed to be quartering his face with narrowed eyes as if he were assuring himself of the veracity of Hugh's response.

"Thank God." Theo's hands dropped from Hugh's face, and he pulled Hugh in close against his body. Hugh was even more confused, but it felt so good to have Theo hold him again like this that, for a moment, he didn't care. It lasted only briefly, then Theo drew back. "We must get you somewhere more defensible," he said, keeping his voice low.

Growing ever more bewildered, Hugh decided he had had quite enough and dug his heels in. "What the devil is going on, Theo?"

"Come with me and I'll explain everything," Theo said, already striding down the walk. He turned back after five paces when he realised Hugh was not accompanying him. "God's sake, Hugh, this is not the time for you to come over all masterful again."

Hugh made a frustrated gesture and joined Theo. "Tell me now," he demanded as he tried to keep pace. Theo, usually so careful to match his stride to Hugh's, was hurrying and it was all Hugh could do to keep up. "Why are you not in France?"

"Courtenay," Theo said at last, and he did not stop looking around the entire time he was speaking. "It appears he is still in London, and he has got it into his head you are to blame for his plight and he means to murder you. What else could I do but return to ensure your safety?" He swung round on Hugh. "And *you*, you great idiot, you not only make it easy for him but you practically *invite* it, wandering off on your own in the darkness like that. Do you have any idea how long it took me to find you?"

"Well, how the devil was I supposed to know?" Hugh shot back, incensed at the unfairness of Theo's accusation. "And I'm not some schoolroom miss who can't take care of herself, you know."

They stepped out onto the brightly lit Grand Walk and Theo made no answer to Hugh. "There's a boat waiting for us at the stairs," he said instead.

"My mother and Sophia—"

"I have men watching over them discreetly as a precaution."

Hugh stopped and turned to face Theo. "You think this so serious? He doesn't have an army."

"No, but he has run mad from what I am told, which makes him more dangerous than a sane man, for he will not care about consequences. He also has friends. I don't know if he could persuade any of them to join him on such an endeavour, but ending up dead because we made an assumption would be rather annoying, don't you think?"

Something of Theo's urgency was beginning to communicate itself to Hugh. As they crossed the Thames, his blood was thrumming, sending a sharp undertone of alarm through his body, because Hugh had never before seen Theo worried. This must be serious.

Theo didn't relax his watchfulness until they were in the hackney coach that was waiting to take them back to Hugh's lodgings. As the hack made its way through the streets, Theo finally turned his attention to Hugh.

"Please have some consideration in future, Hugh, and do not wander off like that again with a lunatic spy on the loose. It is bad for my health, not least because had he appeared, you would doubtless have gambolled up to him like a friendly puppy."

The mockery stung. "I am not entirely stupid, you know, no matter what people seem to think."

"I didn't mean—" Theo paused, then sighed. "You worried me," he confessed. "Your man said you had gone to Vauxhall Gardens and I knew you didn't, *couldn't* know the danger you were in. I was searching and I couldn't find you, and there were the rockets banging, and I couldn't tell if one of them might be a gunshot. You had me worried, Hugh."

Hugh had never before heard Theo sound so grim, and he realised suddenly that the teasing had been Theo's way of communicating his concern.

"But, Theo, I don't understand—why does Courtenay bear me a grudge? And what the devil is he doing still in London? I would have thought he would have fled to France immediately he knew he was discovered."

"As to why he is still here, I can only think it's because we have the ports and the South Coast sewn up so tight he can't get out. Perhaps it helped that I suggested we set a close watch on *all* roads out of the city, not only the ones leading south, after I had heard the detail of your daring plan to set me free."

The dazzling gaslights of Pall Mall shone through the carriage windows, and Hugh could clearly see the amusement that crossed Theo's face as he referred to Hugh's scheme. He clenched his jaw and turned away. After the apology Theo had made to him at Carswell, Hugh could not believe he would raise the subject again, let alone mock him with it.

Theo leaned forward suddenly. "What is it, Hugh? I know I've made a hideous mull of things between us, but I don't understand what's going on in that head of yours."

Hugh shrugged helplessly, for what could he say? Only the truth. And perhaps it was time to have this out in the open, for he didn't understand Theo and it seemed Theo didn't understand him.

"I don't appreciate having my mistakes thrown in my face," he said, his voice low so that Theo had to lean in closer to hear him above the creaking of the carriage. "You tell me what you did was only for information and that you are sorry for it, yet you continue to raise the subject of my susceptibility and evidently find it amusing. I don't know what to believe, whether you were indeed merely spying when you—when we..." He faltered over his words, then decided Theo would understand his meaning well enough without Hugh having to humiliate himself further, and plunged on. "Or perhaps you were instead simply having fun at my expense. Either way, I do not enjoy being reminded of the whole wretched business."

That was plain enough. Baring his soul in such a way left Hugh feeling shaken, but one small mercy was that Theo would never know, for they had left the brightness of Pall Mall behind them and the hack was in near darkness once more.

Theo drew in a sharp breath. "Is *that* what you—"

The jarvey rapped loudly on the roof to announce they had arrived at their destination. "Damn it to *hell*," Theo swore. "Hugh, we are not done with this conversation. You have this all wrong."

Hugh had no chance to wonder what he might mean, for Theo had sprung lightly down from the hack and was inspecting the street around them as Hugh climbed out of the carriage.

"We must get you inside and discuss what to do next. You have pistols, I take it?"

"Of course," Hugh said, feeling mildly insulted that Theo would feel the need to ask.

"But not, I suppose, with you now," Theo concluded, walking with Hugh to the front door of his lodgings as they both kept a careful watch.

"I was attending an evening's entertainment at Vauxhall Gardens," Hugh said. "What do you think the odds are?"

"I think, my dear Hugh, that we need to talk about just how trusting you are."

Hugh opened the door, finding the hall was lit only by a candle in a glass lantern upon the table. "Murray won't expect me back for some hours yet," he explained to Theo as he undid the lantern to light a spill and then used it to set alight the candles in the candelabra. "I expect he has gone to the tavern he frequents."

Hugh led the way into the sitting room. As he entered the room, he saw something from the corner of his eye and swung round, raising the heavy candelabra as a weapon. His movement sent wild shadows chasing across the room; they obscured the face of the man who stood in the opposite corner, but the silver mounts on his pistol glinted in the candlelight as the muzzle pointed at Hugh's chest.

"Theo—" Hugh started in warning, though it was too late. It was far too late.

"Gun down, Lindsay. *Now.*"

Hugh had never heard Courtenay speak in such a way, his voice like a whip crack. Every last trace of studied laziness or boredom had vanished.

"Do it, Lindsay," Courtenay said, "or I will shoot you before you can raise it fully, and you know it."

As the light steadied once more, Hugh could see Courtenay properly. His eyes were trained on Theo, who was just behind Hugh. With every appearance of reluctance, Theo placed his pistol down upon the carpet. Hugh put down the candelabra on the sideboard next to him so he had his hands free for whatever might come next.

As Courtenay stepped forward from the corner, Hugh stared. Courtenay looked as if he had not shaved for some days, but it was the gauntness in his face and the way his bloodshot eyes were glassy above his hollow cheeks that led Hugh to realise this was not the man he had known. He could not be entirely sure he wasn't drunk or drugged.

"What the devil do you want, Courtenay?" he demanded.

"Do you really think me that stupid? You may drop the act now, Fanshawe."

"The act?"

Courtenay's jaw clenched, and the gun that had been steady on Hugh's chest jerked violently. "Damn you, Fanshawe. *No one* is as dull-witted as you pretend to be."

"You're mistaken, Courtenay." Theo pushed forward to stand beside Hugh, though he did not step far from where his pistol lay on the floor.

"I didn't expect to see you here, Lindsay, I must confess," Courtenay said, and for a moment he sounded like his old tart-tongued self. "Unless—oh, God, that's it, isn't it?" His voice rose wildly. "You're in this together! You were there to distract me from the fact that Fanshawe was spying on me. The two of you had me as good as hanged between you. I never had a chance, damn you."

Hugh was briefly tempted to point out the ridiculousness of Courtenay's charge, but found the muzzle of the pistol trained on his heart had a remarkably sobering effect.

"You're wrong," Theo said, obviously not suffering the same concern as Hugh about upsetting the lunatic with the loaded pistol. Then again, it wasn't currently pointing at him. "Fanshawe is exactly what he seems. I'm the one who uncovered you. Fanshawe was simply my dupe. Truth to tell," he said, with a slight smile as he stepped away from Hugh, "he still hasn't worked it out."

Courtenay looked confused all of a sudden, and his gun moved from Hugh to Theo.

Theo shrugged. "He really is just that slow," he said. "You can't shoot the man for that, now can you? But if you're going to go ahead with this, you don't mind if I have a last drink?"

Courtenay began to shake as Theo stepped further into the room. "Stop!"

Theo halted at the shrill command.

"I don't believe you—you're *both* to blame." Courtenay's eyes were moving wildly between them, though his pistol held steady on Theo. Hugh was busy calculating angles and distances, but he could see no way either of them could safely disarm the madman from where they currently stood.

"I assure you, I am the only one who can take credit for unmasking you." Theo's voice was smooth, almost comforting, and completely compelling. Hugh could not understand how anyone could resist such a tone from him. "Now be a good fellow and allow me one final glass, while you let our poor dull captain here retreat from something of which he knows nothing."

"You're lying," Courtenay accused, sounding distressed. He began to move his pistol jerkily from Theo to Hugh and back again, but it was never off either of them for more than a second. He steadied his gun in Theo's direction as he fixed his burning gaze on Hugh, hatred and a sort of wild clarity in it, as if he had finally seen the truth of the matter. "I *know* it's you, Fanshawe! Damn you to hell, with your pox-ridden—"

"The thing is, Courtenay," Theo said loudly, interrupting him without a second thought, a rash act that made Hugh wonder who was the real lunatic in the room, "that isn't a double-barrelled pistol and you can't conceivably reload with any great speed. You have to decide who the bigger threat is here—me, or the crippled captain?"

Courtenay's attention focussed entirely on Theo, and Hugh sidled slowly along the wall towards Courtenay, his heart in his mouth for he could scarcely believe Courtenay wouldn't notice. But Courtenay was too taken up with what Theo had just said, and Hugh saw the instant when he decided on his course, hate and fury twisting his face. Hugh flung himself forward.

His launch was unbalanced, but there was enough force and weight behind it to send Courtenay crashing to the ground beneath him, the pistol discharging as they went down. Sprawled over Courtenay, Hugh drew back just enough to let loose a roundhouse of a punch to his jaw to subdue him. He then realised Courtenay wasn't moving, and it had been unnecessary.

Drawing a breath to steady himself, Hugh looked up, and his heart stopped. Theo was stock still in the middle of the room, his hand pressed to his shoulder, red welling between his fingers.

"Theo." Fear and desperation clogged his throat as he scrambled somehow to his feet. "Oh God, *Theo*!"

The room whirled around him, and then Theo was suddenly there, steadying him.

"It's a scratch, no more," he said calmly. "How does our friend?"

Hugh wouldn't believe him, not till he'd looked properly for himself and seen it was only Theo's shoulder and that the blood was not running too fast. At least, he didn't think it was, but perhaps the tightness of the coat Theo wore was preventing it.

"Let me see," he demanded.

"Courtenay first," Theo said.

Hugh turned his attention back to Courtenay as Theo crouched down beside him. "Damn me, Hugh, I think you've killed him."

"*What?*"

"Well, he ain't breathing." Theo was examining Courtenay. "And that's a hell of a crack on his skull, I suppose from where he hit the floor. It seems you took him completely by surprise."

"He thought my leg rendered me useless."

"His mistake," Theo said. He got to his feet, swaying slightly as he did so, his hand once more pressed to his shoulder.

"We must see to you," Hugh insisted. "Coat off."

"I might have known." Theo's sigh was long-suffering. "You only lured me back here for—*ow*. For God's sake, Hugh, have a little care."

Between Hugh's efforts and Theo's complaints, they managed to remove Theo's coat to find his diagnosis that he had merely been winged was not too far off.

"We must get a physician," Hugh said, unable to take his eyes from the wound, the blood so red and wet on Theo's skin.

"For what reason? Look, the ball has gone through, and the bone is sound, and I think I have lost quite enough blood already. I don't wish for any more to be taken, thank you very much."

The aggrieved complaint in Theo's voice was suddenly the funniest thing Hugh had ever heard. He was still laughing when Theo used his right arm to pull Hugh against his body. He buried his head in Theo's sound shoulder, where his laughter died and threatened to turn to tears.

"I nearly killed you, Theo."

"But you didn't. You saved my life, for had he shot without your intervention, it wouldn't have been my shoulder he hit."

"Well, it's your own fault for goading him in such a way," Hugh remembered, suddenly indignant, raising his head to stare accusingly at Theo. "I don't know why you would do such a hare-brained thing."

Theo's eyes were very steady on Hugh's, and the expression in them was soft and open. "Do you not?"

Everything suddenly made sense to Hugh, in a way he could never remember it doing before.

"Oh," he said. And then, "Theo."

He kissed Theo, who kissed him back, and there was no more need for words between them.

Chapter Twenty-Six

They had cleared up slightly by the time Murray returned home, singing quietly to himself as he let himself into the chambers. He stood in the doorway to the sitting room, slowly taking in the body upon the floor, the gentleman in his shirt sleeves with a blood-stained bandage made from one of Hugh's neckcloths wrapped around his shoulder, and his master, who had red smeared down one side of his face where it looked as if a bloody hand had been placed upon his cheek.

"My sincere apologies for the mess," Hugh said. "Would you be so kind as to send a message to Horse Guards, asking the duty officer to bring some men with a litter to remove a French spy from my sitting room?"

"You may add Captain Fanshawe's compliments to that message," Theo said.

It took Murray several attempts before he was able to speak, but the steel in his character showed by the way he did as he was bid without asking a single question.

"I take it you'll come back to Albany once we're done here," Theo determined as Murray withdrew.

"It would be more pleasant, certainly," Hugh agreed, his eyes on Courtenay's corpse. "I didn't mean to kill him, you know."

"I didn't imagine you did. It's probably for the best. There'll be no trial for the family to suffer, and he's been a fugitive long enough for the French to have closed down all his contacts, so we'd have learned nothing of value from him."

"Why do you think he did it, spying on his own country like that?"

"Who knows?" Theo asked. "Hatred, money, love—any one of those and a thousand more reasons."

It still made no sense to Hugh as he poured them both another brandy. Despite Theo's insistence he was unhurt—it was, he said, scarcely the first bullet hole he'd suffered—he was paler than usual and Hugh was determined that the next morning Theo would see a physician, no matter what protestations he might make.

When the duty officer and escort arrived, Theo was short-tempered enough with them that even the incredulous Guards officer did not dare say too much once Theo had identified himself and Captain Fanshawe.

"We shall see Dalrymple tomorrow," Theo concluded in dismissal, tossing back the last of his drink. "For now, I have had quite enough of this tedious business and wish for nothing more than to be in my bed."

Hugh managed, quite creditably he felt, not to blush at the statement. He held the door for the two soldiers who were removing Courtenay's body, and suddenly realised he recognised one of them—he was the soldier who had been on sentry duty when he'd visited Theo, what felt like a hundred years ago. Now, as then, he looked as if he'd not long woken from a nap, appeared not to recognise either Hugh or Theo, and betrayed not the slightest curiosity in why he had been called upon to remove a dead body from a gentleman's lodgings. Hugh shook his head slightly and wondered just what the army was coming to.

"This is not precisely how I imagined our reunion going," Theo said, as he lay in bed, his arms around Hugh.

That reminded Hugh. “I still have your ring.” He sat up, intending to fetch it immediately from his pocket.

“If you attempt to leave this bed, Hugh, I will not be held responsible for my actions. It has been a long evening, following on the heels of an even longer day, and all I want is you, here, naked, and for the love of God, *not* running about fetching rings. Do you understand?”

“Yes, *sir*,” Hugh responded, settling back down in the bed. “Your soldiers must run in fear of you, Colonel Lindsay.”

“I would hope so,” Theo remarked, as he pulled Hugh close against him once more. Hugh had brought with him some of the laudanum he kept on hand for when his leg was very bad, and although Theo had pulled a face, he had agreed to swallow a dose. Since then, he had become drowsy and reluctant to let go of Hugh. “You do know, don’t you?” he asked Hugh.

“Know what?”

“What you said in the hack, about my reasons for what I did. I behaved very badly towards you, Hugh, for I should never have allowed the two things to become mixed, but you must know that my feelings for you were never in doubt.”

Hugh swallowed at Theo’s words. He had come to realise, after it was all over with Courtenay, what feelings Theo was speaking of. In the light of that, he’d thought he accepted that Theo hadn’t cared for him at the start, so long as he did now. Hearing this from Theo set something loose in him he had not realised was still wound tight.

“I know that now,” he said after a moment, and his voice was slightly thick. “I did not mean it when I called it a wretched business between us. It is—*you* are—beyond everything.” He wondered for an instant if he had said too much, but that slight anxiety faded as Theo’s arms tightened around him in response and he pressed a kiss against Hugh’s temple.

“How is your leg after tonight?” Theo asked after a while.

"Surprisingly well." Hugh was sure it would have its revenge tomorrow for the rough and tumble, but for now it was not troubling him.

"Horse Guards will welcome you back with open arms after this," Theo said, and yawned.

"Perhaps."

Theo pulled away slightly so he could look at Hugh. "What do you mean, perhaps?"

Hugh shrugged. His idea had begun as little more than a passing thought earlier in the day, yet he had found himself strangely reluctant to let it go. "I had thought perhaps I might sell out and study Medical Gymnastics under Mr Ling," he said, and his cheeks heated slightly at voicing out loud such a foolish idea. "He's opening an institute for study in Sweden, you know."

"Oh, Hugh," Theo said, a laugh in his voice, and Hugh steeled himself for mockery. It didn't come. "How is it that you surprise me so often?" Theo asked, and he sounded somehow delighted. "You always take the least expected way, don't you?"

"I don't know about that," Hugh said, "but it interests me, and there are others coming back from the Peninsula who are injured. What you are able to do helps more than anything ever has."

Theo fixed him with a stern look. "You do know that not all of what I do with you is incorporated under Medical Gymnastics, don't you? I am not having you—"

"Of course I know," Hugh cut across him indignantly. "Contrary to popular belief—"

"You are not completely stupid," Theo finished for him. "I know. And just so you are aware, I have never once thought that you were. Except perhaps just now when you would have left this bed. Or when you went running around the dark walks—"

“Enough,” Hugh commanded, and kissed Theo, as well as he could through the smiles they both wore. And then Hugh moved tight against Theo, so he could feel the warmth of his body, the steady beat of his heart and the way Theo’s breathing slowly deepened as he fell into sleep.

Chapter Twenty-Seven

The bells pealed triumphantly from the tower of St George's Church as Major James Fanshawe emerged into Hanover Square with his wife by his side. The new Mrs Fanshawe was behaving with perfect propriety, though there was a delighted and slightly shy smile in her eyes if anyone cared to look closely enough. James, on the other hand, was overcome by excitement and joy, enthusiastically shaking the hands not only of their guests but also of any passersby who had stopped to see who it was being married. The service had been James through and through—he'd been quite unable to wait for the Rector to finish speaking before announcing to all and sundry his intention to look after Miss Drury until the day he died. And dash it, probably beyond, if he had anything to say in the matter.

Once the wedding breakfast was over and the dancing had begun, Hugh stood quietly with Theo. He'd done his duty by being James's best man, and it meant a great deal to him that James had asked. Now he was content to enjoy a well-deserved glass of hock before slipping away to Albany and Theo's bed. He wished for nothing more than to be tangled up naked with Theo, pressing slow kisses against every part of Theo's body, with nothing and no one to interrupt them.

He had just conveyed those thoughts to Theo, whose immediate response had been to put down his glass on the nearest surface in preparation for a swift departure, when Hugh heard his name uttered in disgusted tones.

"Damn it, Hugh, can you not keep Mama under control?"

Hugh turned to find George approaching, his handsome face marred by a scowl. "She is insistent upon me being at home this afternoon to receive some fellow, Esdale or something like that. She appears to think the country governs itself and does not understand the importance of the work I have to do, nor the consequences should I be prevented from doing so."

"I could speak to her, certainly," Hugh agreed. "Yet I believe you will find it to your advantage to meet Lord Esdale. Unless I am very much mistaken, should you do so you will find one rather hefty charge upon your purse soon removed."

"Speak plainly, Hugh—you do rattle on in the most ridiculous way sometimes."

Hugh sighed. "Sophia."

George's eyes widened as the meaning of Hugh's words struck him. "You mean… Damn it, Hugh, that's the best news I've had all day. Not that I object in the least to looking after Sophia," he added swiftly, "yet you would not believe the number of visits she makes to milliners and mantua-makers and all that fuss and nonsense."

Having viewed the very many outfits resulting from those visits, Hugh actually could believe it, but he forbore to mention that to George. Instead he introduced him to Theo, who had been standing quietly by, observing George.

"Oh, so *you're* the—" George started, before turning on Hugh. "Damn it, Hugh, what were you thinking? There's nothing in the least havey-cavey about this fellow. Even *you* should have seen that and not raised suspicions about him in such a way."

Before Hugh could give voice to the indignation swelling in his breast, Theo stepped in. "Captain Fanshawe quite properly alerted the authorities to the unacceptable security at Horse Guards," he said, and if not for the fact this was *George*, Hugh might almost think Theo was rebuking him. "He is also responsible for the removal of a French spy who had eluded all others. Instead of scolding him, my lord, you should be thanking him on behalf of the country and parliament."

George's colour had risen alarmingly throughout this statement. "Yes, well," he muttered, turning away. Then he hesitated, before turning back and looking at Hugh. "You did well, Hugh," he said grudgingly. With less reservation in his voice he added, "I'm glad you weren't hurt when subduing that fellow, you know."

"Thank you, George," Hugh said. As he watched his eldest brother walk away, he wondered when the world had shifted upside down.

"Hugh!"

Theo sighed as they turned to find James bearing down upon them. "Are we never to leave?" he asked Hugh quietly. "I have plans for you, Captain Fanshawe, and you may believe me when I say, most emphatically, they do not involve your family."

Hugh's cheeks heated slightly at Theo's words, but he greeted James with suitable congratulations and allowed himself to be pulled into a hug while James spoke enthusiastically of the new Mrs Fanshawe's charms and how he was the luckiest fellow alive. "And I should make a push now, if I were you, Hugh, because otherwise you will lose Lady Emily, whom I invited precisely so you could press your suit. I would see you as happy as I am."

Startled, Hugh looked past James to see Emily talking to the Rector of St George's, and there was something in her face he had not seen for the last four years. He was still reeling from that surprise when James spoke again. "You are quite the talk of the town you know, Hugh, milling down that Frenchman in such a way. It was most well done, but I had not thought it possible for you with your difficulty."

Hugh decided not to point out that Courtenay had been as English as James was and focused instead on the latter part of his statement. "I suppose it is, after all, a very minor inconvenience."

"True, true," James said, his attention turning to Theo. He grabbed Theo's hand and pumped it vigorously. "I admit, sir, I was most relieved to hear you were not a spy after all. Capital news."

"Thank you, Major." Theo's voice was dry, but Hugh knew him well enough to hear the suppressed laughter deep within it. "I believe your bride is searching for you."

James's head shot round. On seeing Elinor looking in his direction, he disappeared at high speed.

"Dear God, Hugh. How is it that your brothers are so—so—"

Words like *handsome* and *clever* and *charming* rose to Hugh's lips in order to complete Theo's sentence, but he had the strangest feeling that was not what Theo meant.

"*Exhausting*," Theo finished eventually. "Lord Fanshawe is like the rooster who is convinced he causes the sun to rise with his crowing, and Major Fanshawe reminds me of a large dog which has been allowed into the dining room when there is food upon the table. I can see why Wellington gave him leave as he prepared to make his next move."

Hugh looked at him sharply, for he had wondered at the leave James had been allowed. "The timing of James's leave seemed strange to me."

Theo gave Hugh's words due consideration. "I can't be sure, but I would not be in the least surprised if it was Wellington's habit to give leave to Staff Officers in the run-up to actions he has kept secret, purely to throw the French off the trail. After all, there can be nothing more obvious than allowing them leave when the army is idle, then keeping them all close in the few weeks before mounting an offensive. Allowing leave at all times during the year, except when battle is openly joined, would keep the Frenchies guessing."

"True," Hugh said, much struck by Wellington's cleverness.

"And now do you think we might—oh, Lord," Theo muttered. "I suppose I should be grateful you do not have even more siblings."

"Hugh!" Sophia swept up to him and took his hands in her own, a habit she had perhaps learned from Emily. "How marvellous it is to see you, and how happy James is. Do you know, Lavinia is to marry Thomas Ivory?"

"I—no, I did not know," Hugh said, with a helpless glance at Miss Williams who was standing just behind Sophia and blushing most becomingly. "My congratulations, Miss Williams. I wish you both happy."

Sophia moved on to greet Theo with the warmest of smiles. Hugh was thankful that she seemed head over heels for Esdale, for otherwise he might suspect Sophia to have a *tendre* for Theo. He would not have blamed her for that, for how could anyone know Theo and not fall at least a little in love with him?

Once the young ladies had proceeded elsewhere to share their excitement at the wedding, Theo made his intentions known. "Enough is enough, Hugh. We have wished the couple happy, and it is time for us to—oh, *God.*"

"Hugh." Lady Fanshawe was advancing upon them. "I am glad to see you in your regimentals, because you know what they say—weddings beget weddings. I'm sure there are several ladies here who will be unusually susceptible and you must put your best foot forward, you know, to have any chance."

"Mama," Hugh said, aware of Theo about to overflow with emotion beside him, though unsure just what that emotion might be. "I believe with Lord Esdale calling upon George this afternoon, you will have more than enough to occupy yourself with for now."

His mother's bosom swelled with pride and happiness, and she smiled at Hugh. "I was thinking that we might—"

"Mama, I would like nothing better than to hear all of your plans," Hugh cut across her with unpardonable rudeness, "but for now I regret I must leave. Colonel Lindsay is injured, you see, and I must attend to his comfort."

Lady Fanshawe looked at Theo in surprise. It appeared she had been so focused on Hugh she had not noticed him. And then she saw the sling in which his left arm rested.

"Oh, Colonel Lindsay," she began, and it might have been some considerable time before anyone else was able to get a word in had Emily not joined them at that moment, greeting both gentlemen very prettily and begging her hostess's pardon but requiring her assistance upon a matter of fashion that had been vexing her for some time.

Hugh glanced back as they finally left the room, and his gaze met Emily's. He was slightly confused by the very real happiness in her face as she looked between him and Theo. He nodded his thanks for her intervention. Although she would never suspect the true nature of his friendship with Theo, she had nonetheless seen their desire to leave and had selflessly stepped into the breach. He stayed in the doorway a few moments longer, watching as Emily's attention was once more claimed by the Rector.

He looked at Theo, who was also watching Emily, a smile in his eyes as he adjusted his sling. Theo's injury was not bad, according to the physician Hugh had insisted he consult, but it had been enough for him not to have to rush back to Portugal. As Theo had said, a rifleman who can't hold a rifle was not much use.

And so he had been there when Hugh had been invited back to Horse Guards by an exceedingly pleased Colonel Dalrymple, and Hugh had accepted. He didn't know if he would stay—he was awaiting an answer from Dr Ling in Sweden before he made up his mind—but he wished to repay Dalrymple for his loyalty, and the job needed doing by somebody. There was also the fact that selling out on full rather than half-pay would go quite some way towards funding the stable he'd decided to set up for himself, either now or on his return from Sweden.

Theo looked back at him then, and his eyes were warm. "You haven't any great-aunts, second cousins or pet dogs who might be next in line to prevent us leaving?"

Hugh smiled. "No," he said, as he looked at Theo. "There is only you."

"And you, Hugh," Theo said quietly. "Always and only you."

About the Author

Sarah Granger is a sucker for a happy ending. She believes, however, that characters will only fully appreciate their happy ending if they've suffered along the way.

Sarah lives in the Cotswolds, an idyllic part of the English countryside with gently rolling hills, dry stone walls of golden stone and fields dotted with sheep. She has shamefully broken with local tradition by not having a rose growing around her front door. When she isn't writing, Sarah enjoys walking in the countryside with her elderly and affectionate black Labrador.

Her contact details are:

E-mail: sarah.granger01@gmail.com

Blog: http://sarahgrangerfiction.wordpress.com

CPSIA information can be obtained at www.ICGtesting.com
Printed in the USA
LVOW11s1726270115

424567LV00005B/660/P